THE WIZARD OF OONA'S YEW

JOLENE GANZEL DESSON

THE WIZARD OF OONA'S YEW

iUniverse, Inc.
Bloomington

The Wizard of Oona's Yew

iUniverse books may be ordered through booksellers or by contacting:

iUniverse
1663 Liberty Drive
Bloomington, IN 47403
www.iuniverse.com
1-800-Authors (1-800-288-4677)

Because of the dynamic nature of the Internet, any web addresses or links contained in this book may have changed since publication and may no longer be valid. The views expressed in this work are solely those of the author and do not necessarily reflect the views of the publisher, and the publisher hereby disclaims any responsibility for them.

Any people depicted in stock imagery provided by Thinkstock are models, and such images are being used for illustrative purposes only.
Certain stock imagery © Thinkstock.

ISBN: 978-1-4759-8653-2 (sc)
ISBN: 978-1-4759-8654-9 (ebk)

Library of Congress Control Number: 2013907071

Printed in the United States of America

iUniverse rev. date: 06/06/2013

CONTENTS

CHAPTER 1

THE ISLAND

I t all started with my feet. I was aware that they were cold. That was the beginning of my awareness. My feet touched bare wood, and I was standing next to the cot upon which I had been lying. My eyes surveyed the room; a circular room, with walls all around, of bookshelves crammed with books. An open window near the cot flooded the room with pale moonlight, the only source of illumination in the room. Moonbeams highlighted the spiral staircase of metal rods, that twisted up above me, and below even farther. Curiosity drew me up the stairs.

At the top of the staircase, an octagon-shaped room with windows on all sides, housed a huge lamp with the light extinguished. From my vantage point, it became evident that the lighthouse was built upon a small rocky island, with sparse vegetation. Off in the distance, I could make out a thatched habitation, with an amber light flickering in the windows. A small boat was pulled up in front of it, on the only stretch of shoreline that could be considered a beach.

I knew not what country I was in, or why, but I knew my destination would be the cottage off in the distance. My bare, calloused, feet led me quickly down the staircase and seemed to be used to the rocky terrain. I felt little discomfort as I scrambled over the rocks, and then cautiously made my way through the brush surrounding the cottage. I made use of the shadows cast by the few rugged trees, as I approached a window and peered inside.

Two stubby forms were moving about in front of an open fireplace. One, a wizened woman, as it appeared from its mode of dress, seemed to be tending a black cast iron kettle suspended above the fire. The other one was gesturing wildly, pacing back and forth, and seemed to be berating the first one. The disagreeable creature stopped in front of a cage, like a large bird cage, hanging in the dim corner of the room. He commenced to poke at something in the cage, to rouse it from where it was curled up, asleep. The old woman said something, that caused the other creature to turn his attention back to her, and her stewpot. My attention was riveted on the form in the cage, and I strained to discern a shape that I could put a name to. It appeared to be a small child, cowering in the farthest corner of the cage. The light from the fire cast just enough light for me to think I could see bare arms clasped around bare knees, and silvery-gold hair falling down over its face.

I don't know who I am, or why I came to be in this place; but I do know I cannot leave that child to its fate with those creatures. My mind was already formulating a plan. The boat seemed to be the only means of escape, but I couldn't afford to misjudge anything. I didn't even know if the boat was sea-worthy, or what direction nearest land might be. Thinking on the run, I approached the beach and the boat. It seemed solid enough. There were oars, and a mast and sail ready to be raised. Wasting no more time, I headed back to the cottage, my heart pounding in my chest. I knocked on the door and opened it, without waiting for an answer.

The two occupants of the hovel twisted toward the door in surprise, their faces registering first fear, then anger, which they quickly attempted to disguise with civility, and smiles that I can only describe as being rusty from lack of use. Playing along with the game, I strained to keep them from discovering just how little I really knew about the situation I had gotten myself into.

"Hello Sir, Madam," I nodded politely to them. "I'm mighty hungry, would you happen to have something to spare for me to eat?"

I was still operating with the element of surprise, for the time being at least, and they were caught off guard; the old woman stared at me with her head cocked to the side as if trying to decide what her options were.

"You heard the young feller didn't you woman, bring some food." The man of the house and I eyed each other warily. Seen up close, his features were repellant and attractive at the same time, much the way a dead fish left to rot and be devoured by maggots, is attractive to our curiosity and repellant at the same time.

"So you have come out of the tower, have you?" said the gnarly little man, fishing for something from me.

"Yes, I hope to have a look around tomorrow, when it's light," I answered. I gave him the barest amount of information to work with, hoping to lull him into thinking there was no urgency in my visit.

The woman brought a loaf of bread, a hard sausage, and some boiled eggs, tied up in a coarse cloth. She handed me a jug of some liquid with a cord tied around it, which I slung over my shoulder. She made no move to invite me to sit down and join them. I couldn't see into the dim corner where the cage had been. I glanced fearfully at the cooking pot that was bubbling away furiously.

"Stew's not done yet," she said, "needs another ingredient. Won't be done for awhile." Her tiny black eyes glittered amidst the folds of her eyelids, and her nose twitched involuntarily.

I didn't really have a plan for how I was going to get out of the house with the birdcage's occupant. The rest of what happened was simply because of a fortuitous event that worked in my favor. An owl captured a goose out in back of the house. The goose made a terrible racket as it thrashed about in its death throes. Master and mistress of the house ran out in hot pursuit of the owl and goose, and I escaped out the front door with the birdcage and its captive. The cage and its contents were heavier than I expected, but it wasn't far to the beach. I threw the cage rather unceremoniously into the back of the boat, pushed it out into the water, and started rowing as fast as I could out to sea.

From a safe distance, I could see the owner of the hapless goose, jumping up and down on the beach; the limp goose's neck clutched in one fist, the other raised in a curse to the sky. Perhaps his wife would be consoled with a goose for her pot.

The night was still and there was no wind for the sail. I rowed with decreasing urgency until my arms ached for a rest. In the moonlight, on the calm sea, I pondered my dilemma. I put up the oars and made my way to the back of the boat and the overturned birdcage. The creature crouching inside looked at me with large almond-shaped eyes. A heart-shaped face was framed in silvery-blond hair. She was small and childlike, but not really a child. There was something very ageless, and wise, or clever, about her expression.

"Who are you?" I asked.

"Wilo," was all she answered.

"Do you know which way is land?" I asked.

"The birds will show you," she replied, and curled up to go back to sleep.

I did the same.

The seagulls' piercing cries woke me with the first rays of the sun. I stretched stiffly and glanced in the direction of the birdcage. Wilo's eyes examined me calmly. I felt uncomfortable, wondering how long she had been watching me.

"I'm sorry Wilo. Let me release you from that cage."

There didn't appear to be a door. I examined it from all sides.

"You have to twist the bottom off," she instructed, adding, "it's easier when it's hanging."

Once out of the cage, I shared with her the provisions the old woman had given me. When we were satisfied, Wilo stretched luxuriously like a cat. I almost expected her to start purring. Instead she sang a song that started out softly, and sweetly, like a lullaby, but became increasingly louder and more ribald.

"That's enough of that," I scolded, then when her expression turned petulant, I laughed at her. "Where did you learn a song like that?"

"You don't need to know what I know," she replied. "What you need to know is what you don't know."

"What do you mean?" I felt vulnerable, and I didn't want her to see just how confused the past few hours had left me.

"What I mean is, who are you?" she asked knowingly.

I didn't answer, just hung my head. Wilo only smiled.

The seagulls that had wakened me were joined by two pelicans. They headed off in a southeasterly direction. A gentle breeze had picked up, so I set sail and followed the birds until just before sunset. The lights of a small city were beginning to glitter along a coastline.

CHAPTER 2

THE MAINLAND

My initial relief at the sight of land turned to apprehension. The city appeared so much larger as we approached it. I moored the boat at a pier in the harbor, and we walked toward the shops that were beginning to bustle with the rowdy night crowd. With no money, and knowing not a soul to rely on for assistance, I was considering sleeping on the beach under an overturned dory.

Wilo hadn't spoken since breakfast, even when we stopped to finish our bread and sausage halfway through the day. She was now quite loquacious; pointing out this shop she was familiar with, and that family of her acquaintance, and elucidating their strengths, and failings. People stumbled drunkenly from doorways, and pushed us aside rudely as they passed. Wilo, despite her size, pushed right back, and was alternately cursed and hullo'd as the case may be. She stopped to talk with a ruddy-faced, red-haired woman sweeping her stoop. I couldn't hear what she was saying, but she turned to gesture toward me, and the woman glanced at me warily. Wilo waved me over.

"Maeve says we can stay the night," she said.

The woman ushered us into her home, and chased two children from a straw-filled mattress in the left corner of the room. They climbed the stairs to an open loft above, and proceeded to wrestle and giggle from above our heads.

"You can sleep there," she instructed, pointing to the just vacated mattress.

Except for the loft, the home was one room, with a fireplace for cooking and heat, a table and rough-hewn chairs and two mattresses, one of which was rolled up in the opposite corner from the one she had assigned us. A plank shelf held a few pieces of chipped crockery.

"You'll be wanting something to eat," she said brusquely. "Sit yourselfs to table."

She brought us two steaming bowls of something I couldn't identify, which smelled really good and tasted even better. I didn't realize just how hungry I was until then. I cleaned my bowl with a piece of bread to get the last drop of gravy, and looked up to notice Wilo staring gravely at me.

"Yer young feller likes my stew," Maeve said with a wink to Wilo. "Hans and Harvey," she hollered, "I want you to catch me some more of them varmints tomorrow to feed this young man. He's looking kind of thin and sick-like."

I think I probably did look kind of sick-like right about then, wondering what "varmints" she was referring to.

I was bone tired, but I didn't sleep much that night. Halfway through the night I started itching something awful. The mattress must have been infested with fleas. They didn't seem to be bothering Wilo. She slept peacefully with an angelic expression on her face.

Toward morning, after I had finally fallen into a fitful sleep, Hans and Harvey woke me up by shoving a feather up my nose and giggling.

"Wake up sleepy head. We want you to take us fishing. Ma said you would."

A muddy looking narrow river ran along the back of the houses on Maeve's street. The boys each carried a bamboo fishing pole, lines, and hooks baited with freshly impaled worms wiggly enough to entice the most discriminating catfish. I carried some "treats" for us to "nibble on" courtesy of Maeve. When I left the house I heard Maeve and Wilo murmuring together.

After about an hour of lazing on the riverbank, trying to catch up on the sleep I didn't get the previous night, there came a commotion among the houses along the river. I ran up behind Maeve's house in time to hear soldiers talking gruffly to Wilo.

"Don't try to deny it, you were seen in the company of a certain fugitive from justice. Any attempt to harbor such a person will be dealt with in no uncertain terms. You know what I mean," the soldier said, grinning menacingly at Wilo. "If I find out you had anything to do with this it won't go well for you. I will personally see to it."

Wilo gazed up innocently at the soldier. "I met a boy on the beach," she said. "He didn't seem like a fugitive to me. He was very dull. I left him to find someone more amusing."

"Yeah, I guess that sounds like you alright, Wilo. But you mind what I say. This town has eyes. You can't get away with much."

The soldiers rode off. Wilo ran around to the back of the house, her eyes scanning the riverbank. I walked up behind her and touched her shoulder. She whirled around so fast I never even saw the fist that hit me. When I woke up I was in some kind of cart that rocked and wobbled on two wooden wheels. I was covered over in cabbages. I lifted my head up far enough to see Wilo on the buggy seat ahead of me, a hooded cape covering her silver-gold hair. She was urging a little more speed from the sway-backed nag. Feeling she had the situation under control, I put my head back down and went back to sleep.

I didn't wake again until the cart stopped rocking. My cozy coverlet of cabbages rolled off as I stood up, struggled to maintain my balance on top of the rolling cabbages, and crawled unceremoniously from the cart. My clothes were rumpled, my sandy hair standing up at all angles, eye swollen and discolored. The group of people who turned to look at me laughed in amusement.

"What did you do to him, Wilo? He looks worse than your boyfriends usually do."

I met her eyes with mine and we both smiled.

"It was simply a case of mistaken identity," she said with exaggerated dignity.

"Yeah, if he knew who he was dealing with he would have run the other way."

They all laughed again, including me.

"Since the subject of identity has come up, perhaps you wouldn't mind telling me what everyone else seems to know except me. Who am I, and why were those soldiers looking for me?"

The laughter stopped and the group became suddenly solemn.

"I guess introductions are in order," said a tall robust man with an auburn beard and dark hair. He came forward and shook my hand firmly. "I'm known as Raemann Redbeard, and this is my home, humble as it is. You are welcome here. This is my wife, Honora."

A handsome, sturdy woman came forward with a bowl in hand. She had been seated on the porch shelling peas. "We're pleased to have you stay the while with us. Our son, Mathuin, is close to your same age. If you need a friend, he'll be a loyal one."

Mathuin's smile was open and genuine. I guessed him to be a little older than me. A tall, well-built lad, with auburn hair and grey eyes, Mathuin stood to shake my hand.

"Our daughter Cailean is at the next farm down," Honora continued. "She's been wanting a horse of her own since before she was big enough to ride. Our neighbor can use the help, and Cailean's been working off the price of a colt. She'll be home at suppertime, and that won't be long now."

"You have waited patiently enough," said Raemann. "There are a few who know your true identity, some of them can be trusted and some cannot. You are safe here for now, but we can't be sure how long. The less you know for now, the safer you may be. Also, you have been away for quite a while. Forgive me if you will, but we really don't know the true state of your loyalties at this point. There is much at stake. You must be patient."

His eyes locked on mine and I felt an urgent desire to communicate to him just how much I wanted him to trust me. But what could I tell him? I remembered nothing before I woke up in the lighthouse tower two days ago.

"We can't let him go on without a name though, can we? What should we call him? Wilo, you know him best, what do you say?"

Oh no, I thought, please don't leave it up to her. I'll probably be the Cabbage King or Blackeye. I glanced over at Wilo, and tried to smile. She was studying me intently.

"He's to be called Brennan," she pronounced, and I knew it would be so.

CHAPTER 3

THE FARM

Raemann's family made me feel right at home. Honora's lye soap got rid of the fleas, and my eye healed. Her cooking built up my body, and her affection and earthy humor warmed my heart. The family worked hard, and laughed a lot. It felt good to belong somewhere, to be surrounded by people who felt affection for each other. I felt their goodwill, but I couldn't help but reflect on what Raemann had said that first day I met him. How could they know and trust my intentions when I knew so little about myself.

Each day I worked in the fields with Mathuin. I was eager to show him that I had something to contribute, but I really couldn't match his pace, at least not at first. Toward the end of the summer I felt I was putting in a good days work and earning my keep. I wore his hand-me-downs, and they nearly fit now.

Mathuin and I developed a camaraderie that felt comfortable. We shared a room under the eaves, and at times confided in each other at night, before we fell into the deep restorative sleep known to those of good conscience who work hard for a living. It seemed easier to talk in the dark with the stars, and your thoughts, for company.

"Mathuin?"

"Yes Brennan?"

"I haven't seen much of Wilo lately. Where does she call home?"

There was silence for a while before Mathuin answered, but I was patient because I knew he was thinking what to say.

"Wilo's home is everywhere and nowhere," he replied.

"What do you mean Mathuin, why does she have no home?"

"Wilo had a home but she can't go there anymore. You will understand soon enough."

"Mathuin?"

"Yes Brennan," He answered sleepily.

"Why do you think she named me Brennan?"

"I don't know, Brennan."

"Does Brennan have a meaning, Mathuin?"

"Yes it does, Brennan. It means 'teardrop.'"

I pondered this information for a long time in the dark before I fell asleep.

In my dream a fierce battle raged in an underground kingdom. I heard the fearful whimpering cries of children, the anguished sobs of mothers in their grief. A beautiful woman appeared, surrounded by a glowing greenish light. Her expression was calm and peaceful. Her smile brought hope into the dark forbidding place. The warriors ceased their awful hacking and their wrathful hearts turned contrite. Just as suddenly, the greenish light was extinguished, and the Lady disappeared. The battle resumed as fiercely as before.

I woke up sweating and thrashing, my fingers clenched and cramped as if they had wielded a sword in a nightlong battle. That morning at breakfast I related my dream to Raemann's family; my new family. Raemann and Mathuin exchanged a meaningful glance. Honora piled extra pancakes on my plate and gave me a sympathetic smile.

There is one member of my new family I haven't told you about. That's because I don't really know what to think of her. Cailean is an unusual girl, you might say. If she had been born a horse she might have been quite content. She is very opinionated as well, and curious. Nosy might be a better word. It's not that I don't like her, she's all right, but she bothers me more than I care to admit. I really try to be polite to her, because I don't want to ruffle her feathers. The more polite I am the more obnoxious she behaves. No one else seems to notice it. I might have to talk to Mathuin about it some night. I don't want to offend him; after all she is his little sister. I don't want him to think it's important or anything either, because it really isn't important. She just bothers me. I should be able to rise above it. I'm older and more mature; but she really bugs me.

Yesterday I was in the barn stacking hay bales in the loft above the stalls. Cailean was following me around jabbering non-stop, a mile a minute, and trying to help me stack bales. She has her own chores to do, and besides she was constantly right in back of me whenever I turned around. I tried to just ignore her and go on with my business, thinking she would get the hint, but that's just not Cailean.

Finally I stood up straight, leaned on my pitchfork, and said, calm as can be; "Cailean, don't you have some chores of your own to do?"

You would have thought I horsewhipped the girl. She had been looking up at me with a rosy looking smile on her face. Her lips trembled and her eyes, which had been twinkling, got all stormy and misted up. Blue eyes they are, and very pretty. She couldn't get down the ladder quick enough, I tell you. She tried slamming the barn door shut but it's a really big heavy door and it just creaked on its rusty hinges and swung real slow which made her even madder. She hasn't talked to me since, and has been avoiding me all day. So I guess the direct approach worked, but I don't feel good about it. Later that night I decided to ask Mathuin about it.

"Mathuin?"

"What Brennan?"

"Do you know much about girls?"

"A little, I guess."

I told him about my problem with Cailean and how I handled it, and how it had worked out, but not really. Mathuin laughed.

"Now why is that funny?" I asked him.

"Cailean likes you, Brennan, and now you've gone and done it. She's not going to forgive you. I wouldn't want to be in your shoes." Then he laughed and laughed.

The dreams kept coming, always some version of the original dream. The latest dream started out differently, but it ended the same. In that dream, a king sat on a throne. He surveyed his subjects before him. With one movement of his right arm, he sent a lightning bolt that divided the throng before him down the middle. Mothers were torn from children, fathers wept for sons and daughters lost to them forever. Then the battles began raging again, worse than before.

I hadn't seen Wilo all summer. When she visited again, I was surprised how happy I was to see her. I tried to catch her eyes so that I could have her return my smile. She seemed to be avoiding looking directly at me. She directed her conversation to Raemann.

"Is he ready?" she asked, nodding in my direction.

"How will we ever really know for sure, Wilo, you tell me that." She seemed to consider that.

"The boy has been having dreams," Raemann said, "significant dreams."

He described them to her.

Wilo's eyes involuntarily shifted over to mine and focused off in the distance. "The time is very near then. He's got to be ready."

"We're fond of him, Wilo, he's a good boy," said Honora. "I'd sooner trust him than anyone."

"There's trust, and there's ability, and there's courage. None of them have been tested," she said. "You've done what you can with the first one," she added. "Now we have to work on the other two. I see your harvest is about put up. Can you spare both of them for training?"

"We were expecting that," Raemann said, "but I don't think it's fair to ask more of him without explaining his part in it."

"That comes next," said Wilo. "But not here. I want him to know his full history. We'll leave tomorrow, early."

She left without a word to me. When her two-wheeled cart was gone around the curve in the road, I turned to head into the house. Cailean had been standing in the doorway watching and listening, as usual.

"So I suppose she's the one you like," she said.

"I hadn't really thought about it," I said.

"I don't want you to leave," she said.

"I thought you weren't talking to me," I said.

"Shut up," she said. I did.

Raemann and Honora saw us off that next morning. Honora leaned against Raemann for comfort, her eyes blurry with tears, and a brave smile on her face. Raemann's voice was thick with emotion as he wished us well. Cailean had left on her horse at the break of dawn without saying goodbye. She had made good luck talismans of jade circles strung on leather for Mathuin and me, and left them on our packs to find when we woke.

CHAPTER 4

THE HISTORY

In our new quarters, the only creatures that shared our view were eagles. We were dwelling in the clouds; part of the day and night were cloaked in mist. When the sun penetrated the clouds and broke them up, it edged them all in gold, and shot sunbeams through to our towers that looked like pathways sturdy enough to walk upon. When the clouds dissipated, the view of the world below was spectacular. Rocky crags spilled waterfalls to the greening valley below, and met in a river that skirted the base of the mountain. Gnarled and wizened, the sparse ancient trees clinging to the rock walls at the higher altitude, thickened to forest as they populated and shaded the lower realm.

During the day, beginning at first dawn, forty new inductees were instructed in the arts of elusion, illusion, and defense against weaponry. In the evening our education encompassed the history of the Underground Kingdom of my dreams.

The history of the Kingdom preceded recorded history, but had been passed down in legend, myth, and song, for centuries. Most of the others had heard bits and pieces of it as faerie stories as they grew up. Now they were being introduced to it as fact. All of it was new to me.

The original inhabitants of the land were aristocratic faerie folk. They lived in harmony with nature and enjoyed the benefits of their beautiful and unspoiled island kingdom for many generations. Their fate was sealed when mortals invaded the island and defeated the Faerie King and his army. The faerie folk took their kingdom underground, and with the power of various enchantments at their disposal, were able to conceal their existence from most of human kind. They never gave up their claim to the natural world, feeling it had been stolen from them. Unspoiled natural places are still favorite faerie playgrounds.

There are many stories of humans, or mortals, and faeries meeting; whether by accident or through faerie enchantment, as faeries are curious about mortals and not always benevolently so. There are also many stories about ill-fated love matches between faeries and mortals, because mortals find faerie folk to be bewitching and fascinating, as well as somewhat fearsome. It is one of these unions that brought us to this point in time, poised to unleash the forces of destruction my dreams had foretold.

Several human generations ago, a young man hunting a white stag, followed it deep into a forest and lost his way. A faerie maiden, daughter of the Faerie King, had followed him secretly on many former occasions, and had sent the white stag to lure him to her.

After watching the young man wandering lost for many days, the maiden took pity on him and led him safely back to the edge of the forest near his home. Because she loved him she didn't use enchantments on him to keep him with her, but let him go willingly. The young man found that he loved her as well and wouldn't leave her. They made their home among her people, and their children, though mortal if they left the Faerie Kingdom, inherited their mother's skill with enchantments to one degree or another.

The Faerie King did not approve of his daughter's union, though it was not the only one of its kind. He loved his daughter but his distrust of mortals ran deep. He waited with a sense of doom for his expectations to play themselves out amongst his lineage. He didn't have to wait too long, as faeries' lives go.

A grandson who fancied himself very clever at illusions, became intrigued with a mortal woman married to a powerful landowner. Taking the form of a swan, he often visited her as she walked beside the lake in the evening. Thinking she had befriended the bird, the lady knelt to touch his beautiful feathers. The swan dragged her down into the lake toward an underwater cavern, one of the many secret entrances to the underground Kingdom. The woman's maidservants witnessed the abduction and ran to tell the husband, who made straight away to the lake to find his lady's body floating lifeless in the still waters. She hadn't made it to the cavern but had drowned as she struggled mightily to escape.

Because of the unusual circumstances of the abduction, the faerie folk were immediately suspect. Lord Varley swore to avenge his wife's death. Among the peasant villages within his domain there happened to be a noble young man of humble means. His kind heart and gentle ways had won him the love of a beautiful woodland faerie of a very sweet and trusting nature. The peasant folk they lived amongst, accepted them as well matched, and loved them both. They were very happy living their simple unspoiled lives. The only enchantments the young wife used were to make the lives of those around her more pleasant.

The landowner knew of this young couple, and their happiness only made his grief the more bitter. He had the faerie girl brought to him, and while she stood smiling and wondering what honor could have brought her before her lord, he slit her throat and left her blood to pour out on the grass at his feet. Faeries live naturally very long lives, but they do die, and they can be killed. Usually they are not so trusting as to allow the opportunity.

A yew tree grew up overnight, on the spot where her blood had soaked the ground. The peasants named it Oona's Yew, after the sweet lamb that had been sacrificed there (Oona means lamb, and that had been her name). When he heard of it, Lord Varley sent men to burn it down, but the yew tree grew out green through the flames and stood tall and proud as if untouched. The peasants began to whisper among themselves, "Which is stronger, them that kills and burns, or them that greens and grows?" It became a motto among them and a password. The superstitious soldiers never came near it, but Oona's Yew became a meeting place for all who would defend the right of human kind and faerie folk to live respectfully side-by-side.

The young couple had a child, a small son. When the husband found out what had happened to his wife, he found a peasant couple to take the child into their care. When he was sure his son was secure, he went to the spot where his love's blood, and just as surely his own heart's, was spilled. There he carved her name in the yew and added his name below it, their two names inter-twined with an eternal love knot. Then he disappeared and hadn't been seen again. That was fifteen years ago.

Meanwhile, the Faerie King, learning of his grandson's disgraceful deed and all that had come of it, banished all mortals and all half-bloods (or mort-sidhe) from the underground kingdom. His own son-in-law and grandchildren were not spared. They were torn from their loved ones and sent away, powerful enchantments were used to close the entrances to them forever. If his daughter chose to leave with her husband and children she could never return but must live out her lengthy faerie life amongst the enemy, watching her husband and children and grandchildren die before her, one by one, as they lived out their short mortal lives and left her to wander alone. That was indeed what she chose.

The Faerie King's decision to banish mortals from his kingdom, while harsh, was meant to prevent similar incidents from affecting his world ever again. To some it might have been considered the just decision of a wise ruler. Varley, however, was motivated by revenge. It was his intent to eliminate the mort-sidhe altogether. He made every effort to discover them, have them delivered into his hands, and executed. The first to go were those who had been living prominently among the mortal population; tradesmen and women, teachers, messengers. When these prominent citizens began to disappear from towns one by one, the mort-sidhe living in more secluded areas grew fearful and more careful in how they approached mortals at all. Still, some mortals had been friends of long standing, and continued to be.

As the war against the mort-sidhe dragged out into a dozen years and more, parents who were worried their names might be coming up took to giving their offspring into the care of trusted mortals. That is how the Academy got its start. There were not enough mortal foster families to support the growing population of orphaned half-bloods. With nowhere else to turn, parents reluctantly relinquished their children to the Academy, as their best hope for a future. Some mortals were students as well, almost all of those were orphans, without any relatives to take them in. In addition there were those few mortals who, like Mathuin and his family, had rebelled, and chosen to align themselves with the resistance. Instructors were divided between mort-sidhe and mortals in roughly the same proportions as the students.

CHAPTER 5

THE TRAINING

About two thirds of the recruits were of mixed blood, the third remaining were mortals. More than half of them were orphans. Of them all, Mathuin excelled at the weapons training that mortals admire so much. Archery, target practice, wrestling, swordsmanship, knife-throwing; he was equally good at all of them and easily outperformed everyone else. He was everyone's favorite sparring partner. With his help, I became proficient as well, though my skills never approached his. Our weapons training didn't stop there, however. Faerie folk never really understood the emphasis that mortals placed on the tools of weaponry. Most find them to be unnecessary, or even prohibit their use, but feel a thorough understanding of the various forms of weaponry is important to a strong defense. Of course faeries, and certain of their half-blood offspring, have an unfair advantage when it comes to faerie glamour; being excellent shape shifters and illusionists. While mortals are not usually gifted with these abilities, they can be very good at distinguishing glamour from reality, if they are taught what to be observant of. In this area I was able to assist Mathuin, and when it came to faerie dialects I surprised myself with knowledge that I didn't know I had.

It was frequently emphasized by our instructors that knowledge of our adversary was the most important weapon in our arsenal. As a hypothetical example; say your adversary is a dusky elf, of a clan that has a proscription for the use of one particular hand only, with which to do mischief. Any thievery, eye poking, nose picking, spell casting, and evil doing of any kind, are to be done with one hand and one hand only. With the other hand the elf may calm a child, sign an oath, write a poem, paint a picture, or eat his dinner. Now, do you think it would benefit you to observe that elf in the eating of a meal, before you stick out your right hand to shake his in the sealing of a deal, or even just to greet him? Knowing your adversary precludes many unnecessary entanglements and embarrassments. If you have observed his habits and his likes and dislikes, you will find it second nature to avoid him, if that is your goal, or to know where to expect him.

Much of what appears to be magical about faerie powers is really just keen observation and common sense. For some reason, mortals have overlooked this seemingly obvious choice, in favor of the shock and awe of arms weaponry. The result has been massive destruction of lives and damage to the environment that outlasts the perpetrators. We do not wish to continue in this unfortunate direction, but as part and parcel of knowing our enemies, we learned what their tools are used for, and how to disarm them as well as how to use them.

Mathuin was known by most of the other recruits and widely respected. His quiet steadiness and genuine goodness, combined with his superior physical abilities, made him a natural magnet for the other recruits, who seemed to gain confidence in his presence. I felt that being his friend imparted an aura of approval to me as well, though I didn't feel I deserved it in any way. Mathuin didn't seem to notice the effect he had on others. He went about his days' lessons and chores much as he had done at the farm; fitting in time to advise a younger recruit in between lessons, mediating the inevitable quarrels that erupted, or joining in an impromptu game whenever the opportunity arose. Everyone there thought of him as a big brother or even a father figure. One of the younger orphans, a boy named Solomon, was a special favorite of Mathuin. I saw them together a lot, the youngster following Mathuin around like a puppy. His efforts to walk like him, or pitch monstrous bales of hay like Mathuin, provided the rest of us with comic relief. Sometimes I was jealous, and I missed the talks we had under the rafters at the farm, just Mathuin and me. We shared a dorm room with all the other young men now, and there wasn't much opportunity to talk together one on one. I would never have guessed then, that this same little boy named Solomon, would have such a large part to play in events that unfolded later. But I am getting ahead of myself.

We had been at the academy for several months, and feeling the need to touch base with Mathuin, I went looking for him where I had reason to believe he would be doing chores. I figured we could work together and talk as we worked. As I approached the stables, I could hear him conversing with someone. Evidently someone else had the same idea I did but had beaten me to it. It was a boy named Drew, co-captain of the soccer team, who had on occasion gone out of his way to point out any failings of mine that he seemed to be particularly interested in observing.

"You know him best Mathuin, what do you think of him? Some of the other fellows are a little afraid to approach him, but he seems totally ordinary to me."

"Why should they be afraid to approach him?" said Mathuin. "He's just like the rest of us, only he feels a little more lost. He doesn't remember anything about his past and he just wants to fit in like the rest of us."

"Everyone sort of expects something special from him, if you know what I mean, but I haven't noticed anything particularly impressive about him. Have you seen anything we haven't noticed yet?" asked Drew.

Mathuin stopped working and stood quietly for a moment, thinking. Then he replied; "He's my friend, I think of him as my brother. I don't care if he never does an extraordinary thing in his life. He'll always be my brother. I love him just the way he is, and if you can't see anything special about him it's really your loss."

"Don't get me wrong Mathuin, I like Brennan all right. I think we all do, but we were hoping for someone who could make a difference. Maybe he can—time will tell."

"You were hoping for someone who can single-handedly turn things around for us?"

"Yeah, something like that," Drew said.

"I don't think things work like that," said Mathuin, "as nice as that idea sounds. We're all going to have to do our best to change things together. There is no easy way out."

"You're probably right, Mathuin. We should be looking at him like just another guy. That's kind of what I thought all along."

By this time I was wishing I hadn't come upon this conversation and that I could leave undetected. I didn't want to be caught eavesdropping, but I was afraid if I turned around and walked out they would hear me.

When Drew left, Mathuin called to me; "Brennan, are you out there?"

I came out from behind the tack room door a little sheepishly,

"They expect you to fly or something, are you up for it?"

"Well I really hate to disappoint everyone but I think my faerie godmother passed me over when the gifts were handed out," I said.

"Not to worry Brennan," Mathuin said. "Drew got passed over in the brains department."

He put his arm across my shoulders and we walked together back to the dorms.

Later that night before I drifted off to sleep, I thought about the conversation between Drew and Mathuin. The thought that the other boys were expecting something special of me made me feel very uncomfortable. I knew deep down that I was very ordinary. And yet, what ordinary person doesn't wish, maybe even occasionally dare to hope, that there might be something special about them; something that sets them apart, or rather, draws forth the admiration and love of others. Mathuin was like that. I knew I was not.

Drew had said it; the others were reluctant to approach me. There was something about me that everyone else seemed to know or suspect and I remained in the dark about it. I know that my own reluctance to welcome others in an outgoing friendly way was part of the problem, but there seemed to be a cloud of some sort hanging about me that put people off. Mathuin had called me his brother. He loved me just as I am. I could take solace in that, and I could try to be more like him.

Because I am relating these events after the fact, some things are clear to me now that were only foggy then. Some of the gaps in my story have been filled in by others who were present when I was not. At the time, I didn't really understand this war that I kept hearing about. I didn't understand the world at all and saw it as a confusing jumble of conflicting emotions and energies. The people I met and the lessons I learned were like the broken images in a shattered mirror. Now I know that each piece had a part in the efforts that were being made to put our shattered world back together. Soon I would find out what that role was for me and the others around me as well.

CHAPTER 6

DAUGHTER
OF THIEVES

I made a lifelong friend among the students. Her name was Rowena. I felt a kinship with her because I often observed her off by herself, absorbed in some solitary activity, much like myself. She had curly black hair that was cut short, and a turned up nose. Her inquisitive black eyes sparkled like onyx set in ivory. It was whispered among the students that her parents had been thieves; that she was an apprentice thief. She had been used by them to slip her narrow frame and nimble fingers in through places meant to keep people out, and unlock doors to let them in, as she watched lookout.

Wars make orphans irrespective of station. Shopkeepers, scholars, farmers, and thieves were all viewed as one, all equally worthy of extermination. She was too pretty and irrepressible to slip by unnoticed, and her parent's choice of profession made her a magnet for abuse from those among the students who felt the need to impose the hierarchy they were missing. Rowena projected an outward disdain for those who tormented her, and that made her appear impervious to their insults and remarks, but I knew otherwise.

Not especially outgoing by nature myself, I tended to search out places where I could hope to find some solitude. On more than one occasion I had happened to find her in some out-of-the-way spot, alone and sobbing her eyes out. I usually retreated hoping not to disturb or embarrass her. On one occasion she happened to look up and see me standing awkwardly at a distance, and offered up a teary, hesitant smile. Having been acknowledged, I approached her and sat down on the log by her side. We watched a family of ducks navigating about a small stream. I split the biscuit I had in my pocket in two, and we fed the timid birds patiently until they finally approached to take the offerings from our hands.

She admitted that she had seen me retreating on other occasions. Realizing that I hadn't related what I had seen to anyone else, nor joined them in tormenting her; she had been curious about me, and had been observing me from a distance. She had noticed the wariness with which the others treated me, and had wondered about it.

She told me stories of her father, a jovial, reckless man who, while he risked her future along with his own, made life fun and exciting until the day he was captured and hung. Her mother sang like a bird and told deliciously scary stories about the ghosts of ancestors and equally fantastic faerie tales, and then tucked her in to sleep, wherever their home happened to be for that night, and made her feel safe and loved. She was beautiful and full of life until the day she died, along with her husband. Rowena missed them terribly, and didn't care what the others said about them. The others didn't know them like she did.

Since Rowena had trusted me with her story, I felt that I could trust her with mine. I told her that I envied her memories of her parents; that I had an empty dark room inside of myself where the memories ought to have been. I didn't really know who I was and that made me feel as though there was no one in the world who really knew me, or loved me, and maybe never would be. Rowena listened, her dark eyes filled with empathy. She plucked a long thorn from the bush beside her, and taking my hand in hers, palm up, she punctured my thumb and then her own, and pressed the two spots of blood together.

"Now we are brother and sister," she said, "and we will watch out for each other."

She stood up then, as if to go, and maybe thinking how things might be when we were back among the others, she added;

"You don't have to act like you know me when we are back at school, but we will both know, and I will be there for you if you need me."

She turned then and headed back along the longer of the two paths leading back to school. I stayed a while thinking about what she had said. Did she really think I would ignore her when we were back among the other students? I realized that could very well be what happened unless I made an effort to make sure that it didn't. I resolved that it wouldn't be so.

In the next few days I walked with Rowena whenever our paths crossed. I would wave and smile to her when I saw her in the halls. Not so much that it drew unwanted attention, but enough to be noticed. I also caught Mathuin alone and told him about Rowena. Mathuin had noticed how some of the others had been treating her and hadn't approved of it.

When I told him about the ceremony that made us blood-siblings, he didn't laugh, just listened benignly and then said; "If Rowena is your blood-sister, that makes her kin to me as well. I think I have an idea for how we can connect her with a group that can make her life here a lot easier. How do you think Rowena feels about archery? She seemed to have some enthusiasm for it during the last practice. If she's interested, I'd be happy to give her a few lessons that would put her on the archery squad among a group of great girls who would really have her back instead of stabbing her in it."

I just knew Mathuin would have an idea that would multiply my efforts. Rowena went for it with enthusiasm. She was already interested in archery, and to have Mathuin offer the extra lessons was more that she could have imagined. She had some talent, too it turned out, and a deep-seated desire to succeed in something respectable. Before long she was leading the squad and had her own admiring throng of team-mates and followers.

I was happy for her, and happier still to know that she was not one to forget a lesson hard-learned. Rowena was, and always would be, the first to challenge a bully and to gently steer someone who needed help fitting in. There wasn't a truer friend to be found than Rowena, and I was proud to be a friend of hers. Through Rowena I got to know a number of her friends as well. In this way we helped each other expand our horizons and grow in friendships and connections.

CHAPTER 7

THE DREAMS

I'm lying on the beach, fingers laced behind my head, one knee crossed over the other, foot jiggling in the warm breeze. I'm watching the clouds float by and re-arrange themselves from one shape into the next. I'm thinking of a cup of tea, when a fat teapot-shaped cloud tips up on one end and pours out a stream of rain from its spout. It's just a little sun-shower and the sprinkle feels good on my warm skin. Just as quickly as it came, it's gone again. The teapot is replaced by a white fox sneaking up on a chicken, which stretches out its neck and beak and slowly lifts up its useless wings, to become a witch's nose and hat. A big blue-black cloud thunders in and covers up the sun, casting its chilly shadow over everything.

Now I'm walking backward on the beach watching my footprints in the sand fill up with water and disappear. A seagull's cry lifts my gaze. Several colorful fish lie on their sides, bobbing atop the waves, their scales glittering gaily like butterfly wings. I wade out a few feet to the closest fish and turn it over to see if it is alive. Its face is the face of someone I have known and loved. I turn them all over one by one. All the faces of dead loved ones. I wake up from this dream sobbing.

"What is it Brennan?" asks Mathuin, his voice struggling through the veiled distance of sleep to reach out in alarm.

"Only a dream, Mathuin, but such a dream. I swear I can't go on like this knowing so little of the events that led me here. Surely, whatever the circumstances, it would be better to know. If I can't find that out here, then I will leave and find it out on my own."

"Where do you think you are going in the middle of the night, without a clue as to where you are?" asked Mathuin, as I dressed and put my few belongings in my backpack.

I headed down the stairs and across the entry hall toward the door, with Mathuin close behind me trying to reason with me. The door to the library swung open and our headmaster made his presence known.

"What is the meaning of this?" he asked sternly.

"I intend to go where I can get the answers I need," I said abruptly, without my usual deference.

"That won't be necessary, Brennan. Our intention was to lead you to the truth in a manner that would be least traumatic for you, and to be honest, to give you the benefit of our way of looking at things. Your own readiness to hear the truth has made itself evident in your dreams. Your questions will be answered to the best of our ability without any more delay. Perhaps you would prefer to hear it from a friend? Someone closer to the experience?"

He went to the library and gestured for someone to enter. Wilo stepped into the room. I have to admit that my heart leaped involuntarily at the sight of her. The feeling was a mystery to me, having never experienced it before, but the effect wasn't lost on me. Wilo herself was a mystery to me. Where had she come from to be summoned so abruptly from the library in the middle of the night? Where does she go when she is not here? She seemed to be, as Mathuin had said, nowhere and everywhere. What was her part in the story she was about to relate?

"I will answer any questions you have as honestly as I can, Brennan, but I don't have all the answers."

"I want to know who my parents are," was my first question after we had all settled in the headmaster's quarters.

"Of course," said Wilo, "I assumed that would be your first question. The history lesson you have been learning is not just idle amusement. It is also your history. Oona, the young faerie who was so cruelly murdered, was your mother. Your father was her husband, Padraig."

"And the peasant couple he left me in the charge of?"

"Raemann and Honora had charge of you until Oona's family took over. Her faerie kin moved you to the island to protect you. Oona's following in death had come to alarm the lord who'd had her murdered. He was afraid that an army of them, with Oona's son as their leader, would be a difficult force to reckon with."

"And what became of Oona's family then? I should remember them but I don't."

"They were betrayed. Varley's soldiers carried out the orders, but they couldn't have gotten beyond the enchantments surrounding the island without help. The island was virtually invisible to mortals. Someone who understood the spell, and was powerful enough to reverse it, was responsible."

I remembered the faces of the fish in my dream. They seemed familiar. All of them were faces of loved ones; my dream told me this, but still I didn't remember. A feeling of anger was rising in my chest and threatening to choke me.

"I came to visit you and Oona's family regularly, and to see if you needed anything. This last time I came, I found you wandering on the beach dazed; the bodies of Oona's brothers and sisters and their children floating in the shallows off the shore. Your grandparents I found in the lighthouse. They were good people, Brennan. You can be proud to have them for your kin.

The bitter tightness in my chest was threatening to crush the beating of my heart. "If they came to kill me, why didn't they finish the job?" I asked.

"Lord Varley didn't want you killed. He wanted to use you. The losses you had suffered were too much for you to bear. You no longer had a memory of your family or even who you were. With Oona's son as his prisoner, he felt he had an ace up his sleeve, that he could use to his advantage. Your impaired memory, and the isolation of the island, were felt to be sufficient means of containment. The homely couple you met at the cottage? They were there for the sole purpose of keeping an eye on you. They were instructed to make sure you had enough to eat, and to inform their master of any change in your condition. I allowed myself to be "captured" in order to be privy to their conversations. They thought that I was one of your cousins that had escaped the slaughter. When they slept, I would let myself out of my cage, and go to check on you. No one expected you to come around enough to pull off my "rescue" and our escape.

"What about my father?" I asked, resentment rising to join the bitter feeling in my chest. "Where was he all this time?"

"Your father is a good man Brennan. He is helping us in his own way. He has chosen a different way, and I respect him for it. It is part of your destiny that you will meet him and form a relationship based on whatever your loyalties dictate. There is so much yet unknown. We don't know what your mother's gift to you by blood will be. That will play a big part in determining what direction you will take in the future. Our job now is to educate and guide you so that you will be prepared to step into whatever your role will be."

"What do you mean by 'my mother's gift to me?'" I asked.

"Your mother was as gentle a soul as any you could find. Something of her nature is in you, Brennan; her gentleness, and, I am guessing, her ability to unite people in loyalty to her. In addition she will have passed on to you, through her faerie lineage, something of the faerie gifts as well, whether it be skill at enchantments, attunement to things of the natural world, or something else, the like of which we are yet to be made aware. When you are tuned in to this ability, you will know better what your direction will be. We can help you to develop your natural skills when they become apparent. For now, we are working with your mortal skills and giving you a perspective on your background, and what the future will be for those like us."

"I suppose you mean mixed bloods, or mort-sidhe, as I've heard them called."

"Yes Brennan, you and I are a minority in this world, and struggling to maintain a foothold for ourselves and the others like us. The Faerie Realm is closed to us and the mortal world is at best a perilous place. The natural world is our only refuge but it is threatened on all sides by the ignorance of our own kind and the ambition and avarice of mortals. But we have many friends on both sides. Friends, like Raemann and Honora, who have a vision of what the world could be like. Faerie friends as well, like Oona's family, who paid a dear price for their assistance. It's not a hopeless task we have set for ourselves; it only seems so at times. At any rate," she said, suddenly looking very weary, "we have no choice but to do what we do. The alternative is unacceptable."

"What is the alternative, Wilo? Why can't we just live in peace?"

"That is the dream Brennan, but there are those who want to see us all dead and gone, and they won't rest until that is accomplished. We can't 'rest in peace' our way without 'resting in peace' their way."

I paused to think this over, suddenly overwhelmed by the enormity of the task. "Who is the enemy Wilo, how will we know them?"

"Some of them are obvious, Brennan. They are the easy ones. We can evade them, for they play their hand by constantly searching us out. The others are more difficult. They are the ones that haven't yet made up their minds. In order to reach them we have to expose ourselves to the possibility that they will betray us. That is the difficult line we walk. None of us asked for this challenge. All we can do is play out our role to the best of our ability, to make the world a better place for those who will follow."

"And my father, Wilo, what way has he chosen?"

"You will have to find that out for yourself Brennan, from your father himself. I couldn't tell you and give you the essence of the man."

"I want to meet him, Wilo. I can't be satisfied with history lessons, and swordsmanship any longer."

"I was prepared for that," said Wilo.

CHAPTER 8

THE JOURNEY

It was decided that the three of us should go together; Mathuin, Wilo, and I. Wilo knew the way, and Mathuin was a good person to have at your back. Besides, he was up for the adventure, once he heard what the plan was. I don't think I could have made him stay if I had wanted to, and I was grateful for the company. I was serious about setting out on my own if I had to, but the companionship made it feel more like an adventure than a task I had set for myself. It was to be a long journey, first to the low country, then along the river at the base of the mountain (a long way on foot) then back up another mountain pass to our destination; a monastery, now the home of my reclusive father.

Mathuin and I had been training through the long winter, and with spring, the mountain passes were open again. Rivulets trickled down the slopes to meet at the river below, that rushed and bubbled and sparkled over rocks on its merry way to the ocean. We had been traveling for several days in good spirits, camping out along the way. A brief sun-shower sent us ducking behind a waterfall that displayed a beautiful rainbow.

"Let's see if we'll find our pot of gold in this cave," I said, joking, to my companions.

"You really shouldn't joke about that," Wilo said, laughing too. "You don't want any of the Little People, who might be listening, to take you seriously," she added.

"Yeah, that's just what we need, someone else mad at us," said Mathuin.

"Why are they called 'Little People'," I asked, more to myself than to anyone in particular. "My mother was a normal sized person. Her family was as well, from what I understand."

"That's just one of their many enchantments," said Wilo. "Smaller is better for certain endeavors, such as flitting about, or making yourself scarce." With that said, Wilo disappeared behind a large rock, and reappeared, glowing faintly greenish, and much reduced in size, above us on a rock ledge.

"Whoa, Wilo, that's amazing. It also explains a lot, like how you seem to be everywhere and nowhere. And how I thought you were a child back on the island in that birdcage. You really had me going. I thought it was my warped brain playing tricks on me."

"You were so cute, Brennan, your eyes as big as saucers, staring at that cooking pot. I had a hard time trying to keep from bursting out laughing and spoiling the whole thing. But you were so brave, my hero," she said, clasping her tiny hands together over her heart and rolling her eyes heavenward.

"Aw, come on Wilo," I said, "give me a break. Those freaky little trolls were scary looking. How was

I supposed to know you had the whole thing under control all the time?"

Wilo flitted down behind the rock and came back to sit beside Mathuin and me, her normal size.

"I don't underestimate what you did, Brennan. As far as I am concerned, you are my hero."

And with that, she kissed me on the cheek. Then she looked in my eyes and an amused smile slowly spread on her lips, as she watched my face turn bright red. Out of the corner of my eye I saw Mathuin taking this all in quietly.

Some nights we found caves for shelter, other nights we slept under the stars. We saw no other mortals, but we did meet up with some faerie folk. Mathuin and I probably wouldn't have noticed them, but Wilo was looking for them, and made her intentions known. She sang faerie songs that called them, and sure enough, when we stopped for a rest on a moss covered ledge under the canopy of an enormous old tree, we were rewarded. A small troupe of tiny faerie folk peered out from among the branches above our heads. Wilo beckoned them to come near, speaking to them in another language. I was able to understand much of what she said.

"We two are mort-sidhe," she said, using the Faerie term for half bloods, and pointing to herself and me. "This one is mortal, a good and trusted friend," she said, as she pointed to Mathuin.

"We are traveling to meet this mort-sidhe's father, a peaceful mortal, who lives in a monastery in the next mountain pass. We respect faerie ways and do no dishonor to the natural world. We wish only safe passage and warning if marauders of either realm should be near."

"Who are your faerie ties?" the boldest of the faerie folk asked.

"My mother is the daughter of your own faerie king," Wilo answered. "This one's mother is Oona herself."

The faeries oohed and aahed approvingly.

"I am known as Twisp, and this is my wife Toola, and my two youngest children, Twyla and Torvil." The faerie children left the pair of matched dragonflies they had harnessed to a curled-leaf chariot, and approached us curiously.

"It would be our honor to assist on their journey, the granddaughter of our king, and the son of Oona the Compassionate." Then he added; "your mortal friend is welcome by your word."

That is how we came to have a troupe of curious and mischievous faeries as our bodyguards. It was fascinating really, watching and being watched by these amazing creatures. They seemed to be especially curious about Mathuin, and he was good-natured about the tricks the younger ones played on him. Being young, and forest faeries, they had never seen a mortal before, let alone been close enough to pester one. They asked the most outrageous questions without any hint of embarrassment, and they were excellent mimics. They had us in stitches at their humorous portrayals of us. It wasn't long, however, before they proved just how helpful they could be.

We were walking single file along a narrow trail; the faerie folk in the trees above us. Suddenly their chattering stopped and they waved us back behind a rock outcropping.

They went a short distance ahead, and just about then, we noticed what they had noticed; a patrol of soldiers off in the distance approaching our direction on the trail we were traveling. Their sharp eyes scanned the forest floor, and the fauna and trees alongside the trail and beyond, for any sign of their prey. My heart was racing with the sure knowledge that we had been enjoying ourselves way too much, to have been careful enough to elude their search. On foot, and with their wrists tied with tight leather ropes attached to a rider's saddle horn, stumbled two of their captives. As the soldiers approached, I felt my movements slow down to excruciating slow motion. I blinked and the world seemed to turn a quarter revolution before my eyes opened again. At the same time I was hyper-aware of everything around me; a bird to my left out of my range of vision, a weasel with a mouse clamped tight in its jaws inside a log to the right of my foot. The leaves above me swayed slowly in a gentle breeze and then the whole world was dark and damp with the pleasant smell of earth and welcome oblivion.

CHAPTER 9

THE GIFT

I sat in stunned silence for a while, to give my eyes a chance to adjust to the darkness.

"Wilo? Mathuin?"

A soft green glow delineated the walls of the small cavern and illuminated the face of Mathuin and the exquisite tiny form of Wilo.

"What just happened, Wilo?" asked Mathuin.

"The faerie folk and I combined our energies to get you two out of a fix, and just in the nick of time, I might add," explained Wilo.

"Who are those captives, and where were the soldiers taking them?" I asked.

"They are friends; half-bloods like you and me, Brennan, trying to live peacefully among mortals. Varley has it in for all of us. Someone must have tipped his soldiers off about them."

"What will happen to them now?" I asked.

"Unless they can manage to escape, they will be executed. They will be hung and left as examples to their

47

neighbors not to harbor 'greenies' as they call them. Mathuin and his family and anyone accused of aiding us is in as much danger as we are."

"Why can't they just leave us alone?" I agonized.

"Varley sees all of us as a reflection of the evil that destroyed his wife. His solution is to wipe us all out, every last one of us."

"Shouldn't we try to create a diversion and help the captives escape?" said Mathuin. He was standing by the entrance to the cave, muscles tensed and ready.

"My skills are mostly elusive and defensive," said Wilo. "Any diversion we create would be more likely to imperil us. I have asked Twisp and his family to follow at a safe distance and let me know where the soldiers take the prisoners. My duty right now is to see Brennan safely to the monastery, and his father; and that is what I intend to do. Let this close call we just had be a lesson to us all not to let our guard down. We don't have Twisp's family to watch out for us anymore."

We left the cave behind and continued on our journey, careful not to leave traces of our progress for anyone to follow.

"Wilo, just before we disappeared into the cave, when I thought the soldiers were about to spot us, I had the strangest experience. I became completely aware of everything around me, things that I couldn't have been aware of, things that ordinary senses wouldn't have been able to detect."

Wilo stopped in her tracks and turned around. "That's what we've been waiting for Brennan, your mother's gift! I thought I felt a surge of energy I wasn't expecting! Your mother was a woodland faerie and her family would have been the natural choice to help you develop those skills. Since they are all gone, I will do what I can to foster you along. We can practice a few things on our way. It seems that the experience with the soldiers jump-started your senses into higher gear. We can work with that, right Mathuin?" Wilo said, giving Mathuin a wink.

"Sure Wilo," said Mathuin smiling, "You bet."

Most of the rest of our journey through the forested lowlands consisted of long periods of vigilant silence interrupted by occasional surprise attacks by Wilo or Mathuin, whenever they felt my guard was down. Some attempts were more successful than others. Mostly they did a really good job of amusing themselves at my expense, but I did start to notice a pattern in my reactions that I was able to reproduce intentionally, with some effort. Before long I was able to sustain the heightened state of awareness for longer periods of time, and with much less effort. It was tiring, and I didn't want to hold us up, so I didn't attempt it continuously.

Our journey in the lowlands was about to end, and the last third to begin, in the relatively exposed highlands. Wilo seemed to know every cave, tunnel, and shortcut available to us for cover. One night, after taking shelter from a cold driving rain, in a low cave that was little more than a deep ledge, Wilo seemed unusually thoughtful and quiet.

"What is it, Wilo?" I asked. "Something is bothering you."

"Yes," said Wilo, "something is not right. And I can't figure out what it is. I know the faerie folk around this area, but we haven't met up with any of them. There has got to be an explanation, and none that I can think of would be good news."

Wilo remained subdued the next day. She said she knew of a gathering place that wouldn't take us too far out of our way. If we were going to meet up with any faerie folk, our best chance would be there. By nightfall we had reached our destination; a rock outcropping that overhung a massive natural amphitheatre and stage, lit by moonlight. It was nearly impossible to access by mortal means. Wilo knew a way, a back stage door, so to speak. First she deposited Mathuin and me, at what she deemed to be a safe distance away, with rocks for cover. She made us promise to stay put until she signaled an "all clear." Then she disappeared into the dark of the hillside. She reappeared moments later, her tiny glowing self, and was met by several other glowing forms to the left of the stage, in the shadow cast along the wall. Very soon Wilo was lost to us in the gathering throng of greenish lights that melded into a phosphorescent mist at the base of the stage.

Before long the reason for the gathering became apparent. An ominous dark mist that had been hovering over the amphitheater, gradually settled over the stage, obscuring everything in its wake. The sibilant sound of a thousand snakes gradually grew louder until, with a crack that made the entire audience jump as one body, a wizard appeared center stage; as if assuming corporeal form from the poisonous-looking mist. His dark robes were spangled with stars that glittered in the moonlight, and his handsome face bore a malevolent grin. The name Feardorcha was whispered throughout the faerie throng, and struck a chord of fear in my heart.

Feardorcha was a cunning and skillful practitioner of the dark arts, and his services were available to the highest bidder. Lord Varley paid him well because

Feardorcha got results. If it is true that everyone has their price, Feardorcha could read hearts and make the offers that couldn't be refused. You had a loved one falsely imprisoned? Feardorcha could open doors—for a price. Your farm was lost but for one payment to a greedy landlord? Feardorcha could make the problem go away. His price might be information about a friend or an acquaintance. The chain of betrayals would eventually implicate nearly everyone; bringing suspicion, hatred and vengeance in its wake, destroying the fabric of communities, even families. Somehow I knew without remembering, that Feardorcha was the betrayer, and my mortal enemy. Feardorcha's handsome face was the face of evil, and I remembered it now as the last of the cobwebs that bound up my memory fell away. The searing pain of my losses was replaced with the cold steel of resolution. Someday, somehow, Feardorcha would pay in full for what he had taken from me.

Wilo returned to us after the throng dispersed. I had never seen her looking so despondent.

"Everyone's afraid to be seen with us," she said. "Feardorcha's like poison ivy or a virus. Everything he touches turns sick and wrong. His roots run underground to everywhere. How can we neutralize him before he wipes us all out?" Under her breath she added, "How can we stop him without becoming like him?"

CHAPTER 10

THE MONASTERY

There were no more playful skirmishes on the remainder of our journey, just an alert and determined awareness. We moved quickly and stealthily, making good time. At long last the monastery appeared before us in the distance, as if floating in the mist, looking more like a mirage than something of substance.

"How are you feeling, Brennan?" Mathuin asked, his arm across my shoulders and a concerned look in his steady gray eyes. We were resting before our last ascent to our goal.

"I don't know what to expect, Mathuin. I don't understand how he can remove himself from everything as if nothing happened. I don't know what to think of him. I'd sooner be meeting a warrior father than a monk."

"Keep your heart open, Brennan," said Wilo. "He's lost as much as you."

A young monk in a brown, plainly-woven robe greeted us at the massive carved door of the monastery.

He showed each of us to our rooms, which were simply furnished; with a cot, a small writing desk, and a bedside table with a bowl and pitcher of water, and a candle. He told us that the evening meal would be sounded by a bell, and that while we were guests of the monastery we would be required to wear the robes provided to us and take part in the daily schedule of chores and tasks that kept the operation running. Prayers and devotions would be at our own discretion, but we were welcome to attend.

Having completed their task of delivering me safely to the monastery, Wilo and Mathuin intended to leave in the morning. They were planning to meet with Twisp's group to find out what could be done about the captives before it was too late. I felt pained at the thought of them leaving without me. Whatever the ordeal, it was always better to face it with your mates, than alone. The journey toward my father had knit us together in a way that only an adventure such as this can do. We would all feel the loss at our separation. We each had our tasks to perform, and mine was to re-establish a relationship, or at least an understanding, with my father.

As it turned out, my father didn't live at the monastery. A hermit of sorts, he lived in a cave far enough from the monastery to provide him with the illusion that he is the only person alive. I was given instructions on how to find him, and sent on my merry way. I left in the morning, just after Wilo and Mathuin left in the opposite direction, and arrived at the cave before the sun was straight above me in the sky. My first glimpse was of a thin man, with long arms and legs and graying hair and beard, sitting on a rock outside his cave, heavily into a conversation with a bird. He jumped up as I approached, and wrapped his long arms around me in a hug, then held me at arm's length to get a good look at me.

"It's so good to see you son! What a sight you are for sore eyes! Ah, there is much of your mother in your face; her large green eyes, and something of her expression about the mouth."

I was taking a similar inventory, noting that my sandy hair and sometimes ungainly limbs and slight build were gifts of my father. I thought I detected a glimmer of a tear in his eyes. This certainly was not the welcome I had anticipated, and it had the effect of catching me off guard. My practiced aloofness was nearly washed away in the wave of affection I felt coming towards me. Now the hospitable host, he offered me a rock to sit on, and asked me to describe my journey.

"Since I heard you were coming, I haven't been able to sleep for the last three nights," he said.

"How could you possibly have known I was coming?" I asked him.

"I have many messengers," he said. Lifting up his arm, he chirped to the bird that landed on his extended palm and the bird chirped back.

"Don't look so surprised," he said. "Your mother taught me, and you can learn as well."

"You mean you really understand what that bird is saying, and the bird understands you?"

"Understanding what animals are saying isn't difficult at all. It's having the openness to it that most people have trouble with. The animals have to sense your openness. Any aggression, or doubt, or deviousness, or fear, is a block to understanding and openness. Most people can't maintain it for more than a few moments, if at all."

"How do you manage it?" I asked.

"Some people by nature are more open," he said. "But you can practice it. Simply trying not to be negative won't work. The more you try not to think about something the more you actually go there. You have to practice replacing the negative with a positive, until it becomes a habit. I think about unconditional love and picture a glowing light. That works for me, but you can choose whatever images would be good cues for you. Why don't you try it?"

I closed my eyes and tried to picture unconditional love. I was rewarded with a vision of the beautiful lady of my dreams, her arms outstretched and a tender smile upon her lips, green glow all around her. I described her to my father.

"Your mother was as gentle and loving a person as you could find. In death she has become the embodiment of compassion for many who knew her and many more who did not."

"I don't really remember her. Do you think the lady in my dreams is my mother?"

"Yes Brennan, I'm sure the lady of your dreams is Oona, your mother, not just as you remember her, but as she is now. I think she is still very connected to you."

"She was so wonderful. How could anyone have killed her?" I could feel the peacefulness I had been experiencing dissolving into sadness and then being burned away by angry feelings of resentment.

My father was watching my expression closely. His voice was calm and gentle when he replied. "Vengeance,

Brennan, that very feeling you are experiencing right now, is what killed your mother."

I jerked my head up to meet his gaze, my eyes flashing. "How could you let them get away with that? And they haven't stopped. More good people die every day because of Varley and Feardorcha. How can you just sit here in your peaceful little world talking to birds when there is so much wrong with the rest of the world? Someone has to stop them! If you aren't going to do anything, I have friends who will. I would rather be among them doing something, anything, than with you pretending everything is fine and dandy."

"Brennan, I know this is hard for you to understand. When I found out that your mother was murdered I felt much as you do. I was crazy with grief and went out to find Varley and kill him myself. I managed to elude the guards outside his fortress and gain access to his personal quarters. I surprised a young valet whose only thought was to protect his master. I killed him, Brennan, and looked into his eyes as he lay dying; not much more than a boy himself. The loathing I felt for myself was equal only to my grief. I left there and ran for days trying to run from myself, from my life, which had become like ashes in my mouth. I found my way here and a new meaning to my life. Your mother visits me here as well, Brennan. I know she approves of what the other monks and I are doing here."

"What are you doing?" I asked doubtfully.

"We are holding in our thoughts the possibility of peace. We are doing this, not just for ourselves, but for all of us. So that the idea of peace is not lost to the world."

CHAPTER 11

THE GYPSIES

Mathuin, Wilo, and I had agreed on three months as a time to regroup and plan our next objective. My father joined me at the monastery and we spent that time engaged in conversation about the life I had forgotten. He taught me everything Oona had taught him about our connection to the natural world and its creatures. The rest of the time was spent in meditation and the routine of communal living. I enjoyed the rhythm of the days and the simple but meaningful tasks that contributed to our self-sufficient existence. There was plenty of time to think while I worked. During meditation my mind kept wandering to where Mathuin and Wilo might be, plenty of time to worry. Three months came and went and there was no word of Mathuin or Wilo. My agitation could no longer contain itself. I no longer had any patience for the meditation, my only thought was for my friends, but I had no idea how to go about finding them. I decided to ask my father for help. Maybe one of his "messengers" could find something out for me.

My father's connections to the animal world were very effective. Within days I had an answer. Mathuin and Wilo had found out from Twisp where the captives had been taken. They had managed to free them, but Mathuin had been recognized, and a connection made to his parents; Raemann and Honora. Soldiers came in the night and took them from their bed, clapped them in irons, and dragged them away. Cailean escaped on her colt into the night. The farm was confiscated, probably given as booty to whomever had betrayed Mathuin.

I knew that Raemann and Honora's only chance was if Wilo and Mathuin could stay out of sight long enough for them to work out a rescue mission. Varley would be expecting just such an attempt, and would be keeping the older couple as bait for his trap. If no attempts were made at a rescue immediately, he would up the ante by announcing their execution.

I was desperate to join Mathuin and Wilo, but I realized that the only way to maintain the security of their whereabouts was to continue to communicate with them through the animals. That meant further involving my father. We needed to be closer to where the action was, so that we could relay messages and information. Would my father be willing to leave the peace of the monastery and its reassuring routines, and return to the world he had found so repellant? All I could do was ask. As it turns out, that's all I had to do. He agreed without hesitation. Dressed in the garb of woodsmen, we would navigate the forest that skirted the city. My father's openness to the language of animals, and my heightened senses to the natural world, would be our best defense.

The trip back down the mountain, with my father, was very different than the trip up, with Mathuin and Wilo. Most of it was accomplished in companionable silence. There was much time for reflection and observation, and the situation was such that this was necessary to our survival, and ultimately to our objective. Almost against my will, I found myself developing an affectionate attachment to my father. His gentleness and caring, for the smallest of God's creatures, was endearing. His wonder and reverence for all things in the natural world, and his intelligent curiosity, gained my respect. Peacefulness and acceptance emanated from his being. I began to see in his eyes the possibility of redemption for the world that I had lost faith in. A glimmering of hope stirred in my heart.

Our animal messengers told us enough about Mathuin and Wilo's whereabouts that we knew they were located in a series of caves with multiple entrances and exits. We didn't want or need to know exactly where they were, for their own safety. They were attempting to assemble a force, and had developed a plan, to release Mathuin's parents. We were to aid them in disseminating information to those loyal to the cause among the faerie folk, the half-bloods or mort-sidhe, who were mostly in hiding now, and the sympathetic mortals. In short, we were spies. We also needed to organize recognizance missions to discover what was happening with Raemann and Honora. Some of our missions were performed by our animal friends, without too much risk, but the other contacts were fraught with danger. Because of Feardorcha's bribes and intimidation it was difficult to know friend from foe.

My father and I mostly kept to the forest and kept moving, where we were best able to use our skills to remain undetected, part of the background of flora and fauna. We never made a fire to warm us, ate only food we found among the berries and roots, and left no traces of our existence. Occasionally we had the company of faerie folk to cheer us.

After many days of this clandestine existence, we happened upon a traveling band of gypsies, camped out in our forest. The sound of their music and laughter, and the smell of food cooking, drew us near. We watched from just outside the circle of light thrown by their campfire, drawn to their lively exuberance like moths to a flame. One young woman in particular caught my eye. She wove through the clusters of men and women and children, talking and laughing, her bare feet constantly moving, her restlessness as evident to me as her beauty and grace. She left the group with a bag of oats to feed the horses. They were tied to the back of the colorful wagons, which were their homes, and housed their few possessions. I decided without any forethought to take this chance to approach her. My father watched me go without a word.

She didn't seem startled when I approached her from the shadows. She continued stroking the horse's neck and murmuring to him while her eyes followed mine. I had no idea what I was going to say to her, but she spoke first.

"You needn't fear us; we are not friends of Feardorcha here, nor Lord Varley either. Gypsies are persona non grata just like you. We're just a little lower on their priority list right now. If you are hungry you can join us, there's enough to go around; unless there is an army behind you out there."

I waved my father out from the dark and the three of us approached the campfire. After a very good supper of stew and good red wine—our first hot meal in many days—we sat around feeling comfortably full and drowsy. I wondered out loud why we were so easily accepted and made to feel welcome without an interrogation. The Gypsies laughed good naturedly at this notion.

"You don't have the depraved look of Varley's men about you, nor the desperate look of one of Feardorcha's informers. And neither of those types hangs around these woods alone at night. They would have much to fear here among those they have harmed."

Gypsy music played well into the night, for the night was their time to shine. The dancing was wild and the spirit of it contagious. The whirling and the wine made my head spin so that eventually I was content to sit off at a little distance and be entertained. My eyes kept following one particular dancer, the young woman who had invited us to join them. She had me mesmerized with the movement of her arms, and hips, and feet; the flashing of her eyes and teeth as she laughed. I tried to follow her as she wove her way in and out among the other dancers until I couldn't see her any more. Maybe she was tired and had retreated to one of the wagons to sleep, or maybe she had left the circle of the campfire to join a young man she had chosen from among the many who seemed to admire her. This thought made me feel sadly tired and depressed. While I was occupied in these thoughts, and staring vainly at the dancers hoping to see her reappear, she suddenly appeared right beside me and sat down. She took my right hand in both of her small hands and looking up at me, she asked, "May I read your fortune?" I nodded and she began.

She laid my whole life out before me. She knew that I had been on a long journey, that I was separated from my friends, and that I had, like her, no real home. She said that the woman who was meant to be my true love, I had already met, but that I hadn't recognized her yet. She reached out to touch the rawhide cord around my neck, and pulled the jade circle from beneath my shirt. Then she looked up at me and gave me the most mischievous of smiles.

"Don't you recognize me Brennan?" she asked.

"Cailean, is that you?" I said, completely and utterly blown away.

CHAPTER 12

THE ESCAPE

The plan to release Mathuin's parents was taking shape; the participants being lined up. The gypsies were to play a crucial role. The week of carnival was fast approaching. The gypsies would be expected to be there as entertainment, while they were generally not tolerated most other times of the year. Time was running out. Raemann and Honora and a number of other prisoners were scheduled to be executed as culmination of the week's festivities. Security at the prison where they were being held was at the highest level. The air around the prison fairly crackled with the expectation that an escape attempt would be made very soon. Varley's soldiers were everywhere, and Feardorcha himself had been called in to make sure that any enchantments had a counter-control. His informants were the most difficult element to deal with.

Everyone involved in the plan was well aware of the risks involved, and what we were up against, and yet there were volunteers. Varley's tactics had been in play long enough for most of them to know that if we didn't take a stand here, it would be their loved ones or themselves awaiting execution inevitably. Many of them felt they had nothing more to lose.

My father and I have discussed what it is that keeps people from acting in a situation where they are being taken advantage of. He thinks it is the hope that if they are good and behave, they and their loved ones will be spared whatever the calamity is; their passivity aids in their undoing.

Most people, I have observed, only ask a certain level of comfort and freedom to pursue their own interests, and would just as soon leave the governing to someone else. They may grumble about taxes, or conscription, and have vague doubts about how their resources are being used, but as long as their comfort level and their freedoms are not restricted to within a certain range, they will retain a level of loyalty to their overlords and trust that whatever needs to be done is being done in the best interest of all concerned. Losing faith in the benevolence of those that govern is the first step on the road to revolt. A wise ruler, benevolent or no, would see to it that the basic needs of his constituents were being met. That is, if he desired their cooperation, or at least their passive acceptance. Lord Varley, not having a keen interest in the lives of his people, had not been paying attention to the signs. People who have attained a certain level of desperation are willing to take their lives into their own hands. At some point, even a symbolic gesture of resistance that results in death, is deemed better than continued cooperation with oppression.

The prisoners were to be allowed a visit from a priest on the eve of their execution. Even Varley would not dare to rile the religious authorities by denying them that right. The priest would be replaced by a stand-in of our choosing. Once inside the prison gates, Wilo in her abbreviated form, and tucked into the folds of the monk's hood, could conjure up a distraction for the guards. That would allow us to remove Raemann and Honora to the charge of the gypsies. There, narrow false bottoms, (very much like coffins) had been fitted in all the wagons to conceal the escapees. Mathuin had argued to be the replacement monk, but conceded when the others insisted that he would be much too recognizable. My father volunteered, and was accepted. The biggest loophole in the plan was Feardorcha. Vigilant and powerful, he would not be distracted by Wilo's enchantments, but would be watchful for them. Someone else would have to take care of Feardorcha. Mathuin and I volunteered for that duty.

Everyone has a weakness. Feardorcha, as a keen observer of human nature, was well aware of his adversaries' weaknesses. Most of us are myopic when it comes to our own. This is what we were counting on in our plan for "neutralizing" Feardorcha, to use Wilo's word. Feardorcha's weakness was his ego. We started a rumor that there was a wizard more magnificent, more powerful, and cleverer by far than Feardorcha. First just a few individuals circulated the story, and then others embellished it and spread it further. Someone had an uncle who had seen him in a distant city, built upon a great river, turning the water to milk. Others had traveled to another distant location, and had seen him there, performing wondrous feats for the throngs along the canals. We had no doubt that Feardorcha's informants would keep him up to date. Then we issued a public challenge, from our wizard to Feardorcha, to prove once and for all, which of them deserved the people's respect and allegiance. This challenge was to be met at a public gathering place, the grassy area surrounding Oona's Yew, at sundown on the night before the last day of the carnival. Such a challenge at carnival time was an expected part of the entertainment.

We had no real wizard available to us, only the hope that our distraction would give the others enough time for the escape. It was a desperate plan but the only one we had. Feardorcha had no real competition; he had never had anything to prove, but the populace didn't know that. Now the thought in people's minds was that perhaps Feardorcha was not invincible. They began to call for him to accept the challenge. Feardorcha felt his fearful grip on the populace weakening. They were becoming unruly and belligerent. As the evening of the second to last day of carnival approached, the crowd outside Feardorcha's quarters swelled, and their chanting grew louder and more abusive. Feardorcha was not used to opposition. His bruised ego craved reparation. He would put an end to this nonsense before it got any further out of hand. Doubling the guard at the prison, he strode from his quarters, with a small band of the elite guard, in the direction of Oona's Yew.

The escape plan went into operation as soon as Feardorcha left his quarters. My father and Wilo, (tucked away in the hood), approached the first set of guards and requested an audience with the prisoners in the name of Lord Varley and the religious authority at that time, Archbishop Wingate. The official documents of passage were requested. My father handed them a blank roll of parchment. Upon it, Wilo had inscribed (in magical runes) a bunch of nonsense. The bewitched guards would find it to be irresistibly authentic, for a period of time that we deemed necessary. It would then revert to blank parchment. Wilo couldn't resist the opportunity to insult the guards and Lord Varley, in her message, in a very cheeky fashion, which gave her a great deal of enjoyment. They proceeded to the next set of guards, and the next without incident until they were standing before the cell that housed Raemann and Honora. The guard removed the ring of keys from his belt and opened their cell.

At a signal from my father, every rat in the city and his country cousin poured into the prison and swarmed around the soldiers; climbing up their legs, and scrambling up their shoulders. Wilo flew out of the hood, grabbed the ring of keys from the frantic guard, and opened the other prisoners' cells. Then they all made their way, with much haste, out of the prison to the gypsy wagons where they were safely tucked into their hiding places. The soldiers were so panicked that they never even noticed that the prisoners had gone until the rat plague subsided, and then, fearing Varley's wrath, they deserted the prison themselves.

Meanwhile, Mathuin and I were anticipating our show-down with Feardorcha, fully expecting that today would be our last. We knew we had to create an initial impression that would sustain our illusion, but we also knew that would be short-lived, once Feardorcha started testing our real powers. The worst part of that, was not knowing if our sacrifice had succeeded, and what was happening with our loved ones.

I sat upon Mathuin's shoulders, covered from my head, to Mathuin's toes, with a velvet cape the color of twilight. Thus disguised, our wizard stood nearly nine feet tall. Eerie faerie light obscured my face, and glowed from the cavity of the hood, courtesy of the two faeries perched upon my shoulders. It was an impressive illusion, and when we stopped beside Oona's Yew and stepped from the black coach pulled by two matching black horses with fireflies braided into their manes and tails, the crowd grew silent in awe. We had decided that silence would maintain our illusion best, and leave more to the imagination, so I didn't speak a word.

Feardorcha also seemed to hesitate as if unsure of his next move. Then he demanded to know who it was he was addressing. In reply I lifted up my arms slowly and bats flew out of my sleeves and darted above Feardorcha's head, causing him to flinch involuntarily, a sight which drew cheers from the crowd.

Now Feardorcha was angry. Mathuin and I tensed for his next move as he shot his arms forward and bolts of energy flew toward us from his fingertips. Mathuin and I were thrown backwards with such force that we were practically imbedded into the branches of Oona's Yew.

Almost spontaneously the yew tree began to glow with greenish light that emanated from its core outward, to touch the crowd, and upward to illuminate the night sky. The light seemed to draw the crowd forward and propel Feardorcha and the soldiers backward, but it might have been their own inclinations that moved them. Then Oona herself took shape and spoke, her lovely voice a balm to all the troubled souls in the crowd.

"These are all my children, dearly loved, and this my son. They are under my protection. Who would dare to harm them?"

There was no reply as the feet of the soldiers, and Feardorcha himself, were beating a hasty retreat. All but two soldiers, that is. These two hardened members of Varley's elite guard stayed and swore their allegiance to our cause.

CHAPTER 13

THE CAVE

When we met up with the gypsies that night in the forest, and realized the plan had worked, the celebration was something to behold. The prisoners were reunited with their loved ones and around the campfire the stories were told and retold in versions ranging from the comic to the epic. Feardorcha took quite a pummeling for his fear of bats and the haste of his retreat. Wilo enjoyed imitating the soldiers' reactions to the rat infestation, and especially, their awed reaction to her insulting message to Lord Varley. After such a long period of fear and oppression the laughter was a much needed release. Faerie guards were posted around the perimeter of the camp, but no one really felt that this night would be disturbed; not by the frightened soldiers we had seen a few hours previously. As the night wore on, the drinking, dancing, and merrymaking took their toll. A quiet descended on the revelers, along with a realization that Varley would not let our actions go unpunished. Those who felt they were not likely to be recognized, slipped away quietly to their homes. Those of us with a price on our heads, had some planning to do.

The gypsies would be leaving in the morning for the next town, and the next, as was their custom. The fugitives would be going underground, swelling the ranks of those living in the tunnels and caves first taken up by Wilo and Mathuin. The separation presented a unique dilemma for Cailean. Just reunited with her family, she had to decide if she would say goodbye to her beloved colt, and to her gypsy friends, or take up residence underground with her family and friends, as a fugitive. We all felt her chances were much better with the gypsies, but still she wavered, torn by her conflicting loyalties.

"We are going to need someone on the outside, who can travel in and out of cities without suspicion, and relay any information that can be obtained. It's very dangerous Cailean, but you could do it."

I hardly believed these words came out of my own mouth, but I knew she needed persuading, and really felt she was much better off on the outside. Cailean wouldn't have been convinced by thinking she would be safer with the gypsies. The challenge to do something for the group was what decided it for her.

"All right," she agreed, looking at me with an expression that said she was relieved that the decision had been made.

"We'll need to have a way of getting in contact with one another," said Honora, finding it hard to let her youngest child go again to an uncertain future.

A large hollow oak tree, over one of the main entrances to the caves, was decided upon as a meeting place; and waxing crescent moons were set as meeting times. If there was an impediment to the meeting, a hawk would relay the message between my father and Cailean, who kept the hawk's mate with her.

When the gypsies left with Cailean, the last of our reserve of optimism left with them, and a somber mood settled upon the remaining refugees. We moved from the broken camp to our underground home with a sense of foreboding.

Because there were now so many of us, precautions needed to be taken that would prevent our detection. It was agreed that only two persons would be allowed out of the cave at any one time. The time outside the cave would give us each a chance to experience fresh air and sunshine for a little while, but would be devoted mainly to gathering resources; food, herbs for medicines, water, and whatever else it was deemed that we had a need for.

Mathuin and Wilo had already found the caves to be an adequately comfortable place to reside. The caves were warm enough in cold and wet weather, and cool enough in the heat, to suit our needs. With fir boughs and moss for bedding, augmented by whatever we could scavenge for clothing and blankets, we were fairly snug in our surroundings. The biggest problem that developed was not because of lack of resources, but because of boredom and close proximity.

Arguments flared up with minimal provocation. Factions and family groups separated themselves and moved into separate caves, all connected by tunnels. The separation seemed to help for a while, as it resulted in a lessening of the arguments. It became evident that something needed to be done to unite the factions, however, because groups were taking it upon themselves to send representatives up to the surface. On several occasions, six and even eight fugitives were noted to have been above ground all at once, arguing about whose right it was to be there, without regard to what enemies may have been within listening distance. They had narrowly missed being discovered by a search party of Varley's soldiers. A meeting was called in the largest central cave to discuss solutions to this latest threat to our security.

Mathuin and Wilo called the meeting and presided over the introduction of alternatives. Many of those present felt we needed a leader to organize what was beginning to seem like an unruly and disconnected bunch of gangs. Others felt they liked the freedom and lack of authority. A vote was held and the majority decided to elect a leader and abide by his or her decisions. There was grumbling among the few who disagreed. Raemann and Honora were nominated, and agreed upon by majority vote, to jointly make decisions regarding any matters that would bear upon the security of the group as a whole. Anyone who could not accept their authority was asked to speak up. A group of young adults, whose leader went by the name of Wolf, took the opportunity to protest. They stated plainly that they felt no need to abide by anyone's laws but their own.

"There is no saying how long we will have to make these caves our home," stated Honora, "but one thing is certain; all of our actions affect each and every one of us. We can't allow you to imperil the rest of the group. If you cannot abide by the rules we have jointly agreed to be necessary to our safety, you will have to leave."

"They know too much right now to be allowed to simply walk away from here and take up residence nearby," said Raemann, looking around the circle at each of us in turn.

"They will have to be removed to a location distant from here," said Wilo. "Brennan's Island is deserted with the exception of the troll couple, if they are still there, they will have to contend with them. If the gypsies are willing, they can help us transport them to a boat. Since I know the way, I will arrange it, and make sure that it gets done. Do I have another volunteer to assist me?

"You know you do Wilo," said Mathuin.

I realized then that he would have followed her to the ends of the earth if she required it. Their months together in hiding, and plotting the escape of his parents, had forged a bond between them. Mathuin clearly worshiped Wilo. For her part, Wilo was much harder to read. Wilo was practiced at reading men's motives and using their fascination with her to her advantage. Could it be that Wilo had allowed herself the luxury of loving someone? I thought I caught a softness in her features when she and Mathuin were talking and laughing together, a relaxing into a moment's ease that she hadn't allowed herself before. Then the old Wilo would return, with her air of confident command and her irreverent sense of humor.

Wolf's gang of three young men, and an equal number of young women, seemed intrigued with the idea of having an island of their own. It seemed a fair enough alternative for a bunch of individuals who had no interest in the common good. They would have to make do on their own with their own and the island's resources to sustain them. Clearly Wilo would need another volunteer, and I was more than willing to resume our comradeship. I was also aware of the fact that we would be traveling across country with the gypsies and Cailean, of course. The waning crescent moon was only a few days away. Cailean would be making her first visit since the night of our victory celebration.

My father and I had found sleeping spaces near each other, in tunnels not far off of the central cave that Raemann and Honora had chosen. Roots of a tree formed a domed and beamed ceiling, and up through a hollow knot in the tree high above me, I could see stars between the branches of the tree as they moved to the rhythm of the wind. I liked having that small window to the heavens. It seemed my thoughts could soar there as they couldn't in a space that was all enclosed. At night I sorted through my life to make sense of it and tried to imagine where events were leading me and what my purpose was.

I thought of the nights spent in the same room with Mathuin and how comfortable it had felt having him to talk to. I thought of my father and wondered if he regretted coming with me. I thought of Cailean and smiled to remember her earnest face looking up at me in the hayloft. That seemed so long ago now. I remembered so many things that had been long forgotten. I remembered my mother smiling and holding out her arms to me. I remembered happy days on the island with my cousins and grandparents. I wanted those days back but realized that I would have to be comforted with their memory. I felt truly blessed to have the memories back. Those nights in the cave I relived all my forgotten memories over and over. Every once in a while I would be rewarded with a new one to add to the growing list. I would drift off to sleep in the midst of a beautiful memory, and for awhile, in that space between waking and sleeping, I was really there, with all the people I loved. There was no time or space separating us. I didn't want to resume my life, only to stay with them forever.

Eventually I would fall asleep and the sound of distant marching would resume and then grow louder and the cries of battle nearer. I heard children crying and I saw the fearsome hatred on the faces of men. One of the children cried, "Mother, help us!" and the child was me, and the mother, Oona.

CHAPTER 14

THE FOXES

My father and I took our visits above ground together. It was a good way to practice our unique communication skills, which seemed to complement each other so well. Any doubts that I had about him, and his courage or dedication to the survival of the outcasts, was a thing of the past. My admiration for him had grown daily to the point that I respected him to the highest degree. One day when we were above ground together, I ventured to ask him the question that had been bothering me for several weeks. I wanted to know if he regretted leaving the peace of the monastery and subsequently becoming a fugitive like the rest of us. He answered me in these words:

"I have been a fugitive since the day your mother was killed, Brennan. I haven't betrayed my beliefs in any way since I left the monastery, but have acted on them in every decision I have made since then. I haven't ceased my prayers for a peaceful solution. What I have gained, is the one thing that I was beginning to despair of, and that is my relationship with my son. For that I never cease to give thanks to the Creator and to Oona for bringing my son back to me."

He said this with such heartfelt conviction, and genuine emotion, that I was at a loss for words. All I could do was throw my arms around him and sob great heaving waves of grief and joy together, until there were no tears left to cry. Since that day there has been no shadow of separation between us. Before there was doubt and misunderstanding in the words we spoke to each other, making every communication an effort. Now there was clarity and trust.

This particular day we had spent stocking our supplies of medicinal herbs; shepherds purse to stanch the flow of blood, Queen Anne's lace for its worm expelling properties, yarrow for stomach ache and as an eyewash, raspberry leaves for cankers and sore throats, Hawthorne and digitalis for heart ailments, willow bark for arthritis. We were a small number of people really, but each had brought their own particular brand of problems with them, and the damp cave life and lack of nutritional variety was taking its toll. We had good luck filling our pouches with our neighbors' requests and were reveling in the fresh air, sunshine, and frenetic activity of the world above ground.

Not far from the mossy hummock where I was relaxing, was a fox's den. I had been observing it with delight, as the kits popped in and out, wrestling with each other, and exploring the perimeters of the den, while their mother was out fetching something for supper. I was pretty sure I had heard her warn them to stay inside and out of sight while she was gone. But they were young and unafraid and had been cooped up too long. I knew just how they felt. I was enjoying their gamboling until I got a sensation that something was amiss. I yelped at the kits to duck for cover and they scampered right into their den. That was just before I spotted a badger approaching from several yards off, but too close to the den for comfort. The den would provide no protection for the kits from a badger.

My father summed the situation up and addressed the badger;

"Might I prevail upon you, Mr. Badger, with all due respect, to consider the tender age and inexperience of the young foxes and call upon your sense of fair play?"

The badger merely looked up and snorted. "And why would I want to do that? You must have me confused with someone who cares."

"Well perhaps then you would consider that you would be making a formidable enemy of their mother who would not take kindly to you making a snack of her precious children."

"I suppose she'd have to catch me first, wouldn't she? I don't see her around here. I guess she should have been more careful. What's it to you two anyway, I thought you people were omnivores. Live and let live I say, or maybe I should say eat and let eat?"

He chuckled at that and moved closer to the entrance to the den.

"You really don't want to do that," I said, standing up and brandishing my heavy walking stick above my head, as I approached the badger, which snarled and ducked into the den and reemerged with a struggling kit in his jaws.

I swung my heavy walking stick at the badger's back and struck him a heavy blow. He dropped the kit and sank his sharp teeth into the stick instead. The mother fox heard the commotion and closed ranks on the badger, who decided he was outnumbered, and waddled away as fast as his short legs would carry him, muttering insults all the way.

The vixen had found her injured kit and was licking its wounds and trying to get it to eat the shrew she had brought back to feed her young ones. I asked her if she would mind if I took a look at the young one's wounds. She let me take the tiny fox from her and hovered about as I examined it. The largest wound was a deep gash by its neck and shoulder that would need to be stitched. There were a couple of puncture wounds that would heal alright if they were cleaned properly. I told her I could stitch the wound, and that I didn't think the kit would live if the wound wasn't tended to. Reluctantly the mother fox agreed to let me take her young one back to the cave. I told her she and the other kits were welcome too. I hoped none of the other outcasts would mind, but I was afraid the badger would come back for another kit now that he knew where the den was.

I carried the wounded kit in a sling around my neck and the vixen and the other three kits followed. My father took up the rear to make sure no stragglers were left behind.

Not everyone was thrilled about sharing the cave with a family of foxes, but the children thought it was a great idea. The mother fox seemed satisfied that her kits would be safe with me, and eventually won over the reluctant adults by exhibiting her really superlative parenting skills. Her children were much better behaved than the majority of the mortal and mort-sidhe offspring. By night the vixen would hunt and bring back mice and voles to feed her family. By day she mostly napped fitfully until she became accustomed to the care the children provided, supervised by me. The four kits were given the names Flit, Finn, Flann and Flossy, and they kept the otherwise bored children entertained to such an extent that their parents came to be most grateful for their presence.

Flit, the injured fox, was the smallest and much doted on while the injured shoulder slowly healed. Finn was the largest and most adventurous. Flann was curious and enjoyed stalking spiders and centipedes and then eating them, to the awe and disgust of the children. And Flossy was gentle and somewhat shy with a beautiful fluffy tail.

A couple of weeks went by and the vixen began to take her children out for short hunting excursions and various lessons in the school of nature. Flit was still too weak to follow them and I know the vixen worried that her smallest kit wouldn't be able to take care of himself. One of the mort-sidhe children, a niece of Wilo, was a small redhead with delicate features like a fox. She was especially fond of Flit. Her name was Fiona and she loved to sit near the little fox and sing to him. She would coax Flit out of the cozy nest the children had made for him, by leading a cricket around on a string in front of him, and tempting him out to move his sore shoulder in pursuit of the cricket. I had been wondering what to do with the injured littlest fox when the time came to leave with Wilo and Mathuin, and decided to ask Fiona if she would watch out for him. She looked up at me and smiled her pixie smile and nodded eagerly. I knew Flit would be in good hands.

The meeting with Cailean was just a matter of days away. Wolf and his bunch had packed what they felt would be essential to their existence on the island. Wilo had given them an idea of what the island provided. They seemed excited with the prospect of life above ground on an island of their own. For our part, we didn't really view them as outlaws as long as they were making the trip of their own free will. We intended to part on good terms as long as they didn't change their minds. A lot could happen between here and there.

When Cailean did arrive, it was with three gypsy wagons, and a small group of her friends. They would be meeting up with the entire group at the next carnival. The gypsies were under more than the usual amount of suspicion themselves. They were willing to take the risk of transporting us if we could lessen it somewhat by learning to blend in. We were all given a crash course in gypsy dialect, dress, and entertainment. Those with less talent for it were urged to remain inconspicuous, or better yet, out of sight, since gypsies aren't really known for being inconspicuous.

Cailean and the gypsies brought with them news of the outside world that they had been able to gather. After the prison break Varley was in a towering rage. Someone had to be held responsible, but the soldiers who allowed the escape were nowhere to be found. Varley had renewed his efforts to capture and eliminate the mort-sidhe by rounding them up wherever his men found them. He and Feardorcha parted company but both of them wanted revenge for the humiliation they had suffered at our hands. They would find a use for each other when it suited their own purposes. The wizard we had invented had taken hold in the popular imagination. A repeat performance was expected at any time. This information we might be able to use to our advantage, but we couldn't expect to be so lucky a second time.

We had Raemann and Honora back with us but we were no closer to a peaceful solution than we had been before. It seemed that nothing we could do would provide us with the opportunity to pursue our lives without the threat of annihilation.

CHAPTER 15

THE KISS

In the months since she had made the gypsies her second family, Cailean had changed a lot. The traveling life of the gypsies is a difficult one. They get by because they are resourceful and because they stick together. Although they value their freedom above all else, and do not feel bound by conventional morality, they live by a strict code of their own. Cailean had earned their respect and their affection. This was no small feat in and of itself. I had to smile to myself when I thought of the Cailean and Brennan of not so very long ago.

If I was having trouble deciding what to make of the "kid sister" Cailean in a confident young woman's body, it was evident that other young men in the caravan had no such conflict of interest issues to deal with. Cailean was now accustomed to their jockeying for her attention and was finding a certain amount of humor in it. She appeared not to take herself too seriously, which I thought especially appealing. I was hoping she wouldn't take any of them too seriously either.

Wolf's pack of six hopeful island-dwellers really enjoyed playing at being gypsies. With a little assistance the girls seemed to take naturally to the knack of combining anything outdated but colorful, with something altogether mismatched, adding some lace and ribbon, and coming up with something fetching. They were learning to dance and play the tambourine, an instrument that could double as collection plate. Wolf was working up an act that included knife throwing but was having trouble getting volunteers to act as targets. The gypsies knew that part of their appeal to the repressed throngs that came to be entertained by them was the idea of unbridled sexuality hinted at in the dancing and flirting. In actuality they had stricter rules imposed from within than from without about crossing that boundary with the townspeople.

Wilo and Mathuin hoped to attract as little attention to themselves as possible by attending to the more mundane tasks of daily life encountered by people who made a life of traveling. Having been raised on a farm, Mathuin was skilled at fixing anything and made himself very useful maintaining the wagons. Wilo had a talent for painting, and the gypsies were a people whose tastes, if unorthodox, were not lacking in imagination and originality. They appreciated her whimsical and colorful designs. One thing more I noticed. It was interesting to me to observe Wilo with the children. I hadn't had an opportunity to see her interact with children before. I don't know if she'd had the opportunity before. The children loved her. They followed her everywhere. Her attention to them seemed to come as naturally to her as flight does to a bird. Mathuin loved to watch her with the children. He would pause in his work to watch them with an expression of serene contentment tinged with longing. I'm certain he wasn't aware just how much of what he felt he gave away without a word or a gesture.

I found myself thinking about the subject of love and wondering how it fit into the current scheme of things. Could any of us really afford to be squandering our mental and physical resources on something that seemed to me, at one moment to be totally self-indulgent, and at another to be totally selfless? And yet I saw it happening all around me. The incidence of it seemed to grow in direct proportion to the threat we experienced, almost as if it was nature's way of balancing the scales of misery to joy, or more practically, death to birth. At any rate there didn't appear to be any way to prevent it, nor any compelling reason to do so.

The gypsies were very good at foraging for themselves but it was necessary to procure some items from the townspeople. This is where trouble often developed, and for this reason someone with a cool head and non-volatile nature was required. After some discussion it was decided that I was that person. Like Mathuin and Wilo, I had a price on my head, but unlike them, few people knew what I looked like. I agreed to go. I wanted primarily an opportunity to find out what was being talked about among the townspeople. In addition, we were all getting a little tired of the gypsy stew, which consisted primarily of fish or mussels, plus an occasional chicken that wandered too far a field, and whatever foraged herbs and vegetables were to be found. I hoped to spice up our cuisine a little if possible. Cailean surprised me by requesting to go along.

We were camped just inside the forest only a couple miles from the nearest town. Cailean and I dressed as inconspicuously as possible and took knapsacks to carry our purchases back with us. We took up a collection of coins and brought along mushrooms to sell or trade as well as some of the rarer and more sought after herbs.

We set off down the road, Cailean walking along beside me chatting happily. It was a beautiful summer morning. One of the kinds of days that you remember; not for the activity that you do, but more because of a rare combination of mood, clarity, atmosphere and companionship. I was thinking that if I needed a day to remember in the future, a day that you might call a perfect day, when I was perfectly happy, this would be it.

"Brennan is enjoying himself today," Cailean said, "I wonder what that means?"

"A day like today makes me feel hopeful that there will be more days like today," I responded.

"Living with the gypsies changed how I look at things," Cailean said. "They enjoy life one day at a time. After all, none of us has a guarantee of any more than that."

"I wish I could look at life that way," I said. "I can't seem to maintain a positive outlook for more than just a few fleeting moments."

"Well then, as your doctor, I recommend that you have an extended stay with the gypsies. That will cure what ails you," said Cailean.

"You think so?" I asked.

"Yes, I do. You are entirely too serious Brennan. You have seen too much sadness. It's time you started having some fun."

With that said, she grabbed my hat and took off down the road with it as fast as a young deer. I took off after her and she veered off the road toward a lone oak tree with huge sweeping arms standing in the middle of a field. She climbed it as easily as a cat and sat leaning against a limb, a saucy look on her face, twirling my hat around her finger.

"Come on up, Brennan, the view is beautiful from up here."

"It certainly is," I said, smiling up at her.

"Why Brennan, are you flirting with me?" she asked.

"No," I said, climbing up to her in a few quick moves, and looking into her lovely eyes; "but I think I'm going to kiss you."

The change in our relationship had taken place so naturally, so easily, that it felt like nothing needed to be said. We wended our way through the stalls of the market place, examining the produce with the elaborate attention we wanted to devote to each other. Occasionally our arms would brush together and our fingers would twine around each other's for a few exquisite moments until we pretended to concentrate on the finer points of a melon or tuber. We didn't want to be too obvious, you understand. Somehow such a thing as young love is not an easy thing to hide, however. People seemed to take vicarious pleasure in our happiness, as if remembering their own experiences through us, or if not so lucky, imagining themselves in our place.

"Would the young gentleman care to buy a posy for the lovely young lady?" asked a nearly toothless old woman.

I couldn't resist, thereby establishing us as easy marks. We had everyone from jewelers to portrait painters plying us with their wares. We ducked into an inn for a chance to regain command of our bargaining skills.

We took a table at the back of the inn in a dim corner and ordered something to slake our thirst. Before long two men entered, and not taking any notice of us, they took a large circular table at the center of the room. Soon they were joined by several others. They ordered a round of ale, then another. The conversation turned to Lord Varley and our attention was riveted.

"He figures the fugitives are hiding out in the forest somewhere because all of the ships are being checked before they depart so they can't have escaped, and they've searched all the houses from the smallest hovel to the grandest manor. They've rounded up a few but most are still unaccounted for. It's almost as if the earth has swallowed them up." This was spoken by a man in a well-made but threadbare and filthy suit.

"Or maybe like something in the forest swallowed them up, more like it. You won't catch the likes of me tromping around in that forest, especially not at night," another man said.

"All manner of unnatural things is in the forest," said a third man.

"Well here's the deal," the first man said, "Varley wants to put dogs on their trail. He's willing to set a few worthy men up with a small fortune each to take the dogs in after them and be done with them."

"Why doesn't he just have the soldiers go in with the dogs?" one of them asked.

"The soldiers will be waiting for them when the dogs flush them out," said the first man. "Varley figures they will be less likely to be suspicious if it's just a few men out hunting rabbits with their dogs. Wicked plan isn't it?" the man said, with a grin that showed his misshapen teeth and his eagerness to enjoy the sport.

"I'm in it with my dog Stump, any other takers?"

"No way, I'm not going in there, not for enough gold to fill up my pockets."

"Too bad you feel that way," said the first man. "Varley said to make sure the only ones that know about it are in on it, if you know what I mean."

With that he pulled out a knife and put it through the resister's heart.

"What say the rest of you?"

"We're in!" they all said in a chorus.

The conspirators left in a hurry escorting the body out between them as if he were a mate that had too much to drink. Cailean and I waited until the place was clear and then took a back door out through the kitchen. We made our purchases quickly trying to recapture some of our original appearance of lightheartedness so as not to make ourselves suspicious. Our one thought was to get back to camp so we could tell the others.

Wolf's gang was more determined than ever to get to the island. They weren't willing to turn around and go back with us to warn the cave dwellers.

"All ships are being searched," Cailean warned. "It doesn't seem like a good idea any more, it's too risky."

"Risky is what I call being trapped by dogs in a rabbit hole with soldiers waiting for us to emerge. I'd rather take my chances with the ship," said Wolf.

"I'm with him," said the young woman at his side. "I've had enough of living underground. I'm not going back. We will steal a boat if we have to." There were murmurs of assent from the rest of his crew.

"Cailean and I have to go back. What about you, Mathuin and Wilo? It seems our plans have changed."

"Plans have changed and priorities have changed," said Wilo, and then, addressing Wolf's group; "You leave me little choice but to let you go and trust to your loyalty and your own devices. I will show you where you will be most likely to acquire a boat. Let me draw you a map. Once you've secured a vessel, Cailean's hawk will show you the way to the island. You are on your own now, good luck to you. May we meet again under better circumstances."

We parted company with Wolf's gang and the gypsies and headed back through the forest moving quickly through the day and the night, hoping that we wouldn't be too late.

CHAPTER 16

THE HUNT

Fiona and the little injured fox had become fast friends. Flit's wounds healed without any ill effects and the four siblings were growing fast. By summer's end they would be setting off to make their own way in the world, but for now they were satisfied to call our series of caves and tunnels their home. Now that Flit was bigger and stronger, Fiona no longer carried him around. Instead, sometimes Flit would carry Fiona on his back, as Fiona had the gift of miniaturization just as her aunt Wilo had. In her tiny form, Fiona would perch behind Flit's head, grasping the thick fur around his neck right up close where she could whisper in Flit's ear and be easily heard. This way they could travel around together and talk if they liked or, as was more often the case, just enjoy each other's company as they learned about the world around them together. When it was Fiona's turn to be above ground she could most often be found in the company of her friend Flit.

We arrived back at the cave before first light. As I had mentioned earlier, night was not a frightening time for the fugitives in the forest. We felt safest then, for our enemies were not the animals, nor were they the things of the imagination that the soldiers and townspeople feared. They feared the wraiths and spirits, the little people and the gypsies, because they knew them not. With most of that company as friends and fellow travelers, we had much less to fear of the night; the night kept our enemies at bay. Now that we had delivered our warning there was nothing to do but wait for the dawn and the hunters.

The mother fox had some experience with men and dogs. She told her children to stay in the cave, no matter what; "They can't track you down if you stay hidden and don't move," she said.

We took some precautions by rolling stones over some of the larger entrances. We covered track marks and disguised the smaller exits with brush. No fires were lit for cooking. No one had slept much so most of us were awake to hear the baying of the dogs as they approached. They made several passes near our tunnels without pausing. Then there was a ruckus near one of the small exits. A rat terrier had entered a tunnel and was approaching the main cave where most of the fugitives, including the young foxes, were huddled for protection. Before the terrier could reach the main cave, the mother fox dashed past him and led him out another exit. He barked up a storm as he followed in pursuit, attracting the attention of the hunters whose dogs set off after her.

"False alarm lads, this is nothing but a fox's den," said the man with the misshapen teeth. "I've been hankering for a fox tail for my hat, let's have us a little sport!"

With that they set off in pursuit of the mother fox and left us to wonder and worry and feel relieved all at one time.

"Don't worry Flit," said Fiona. "Your mother is very fast and very smart."

"But there are so many dogs," said Flit. "Mother doesn't like dogs."

"And they have guns," said Finn, with a worried shake of his head.

Off in the distance came the sound of gunshots and the raucous barking of the dogs.

The mother fox didn't return that night. We tried to reassure ourselves, and the young foxes, that she had found a hiding place and would return when it was all clear. But when we didn't see her the next day either, or the next, it became evident that she wouldn't be coming back. Flit and Fiona went out with Finn looking for her several nights in a row. They worried she had been hurt and couldn't make it home alone. Flann and Flossy cried themselves into fitful sleep and wandered about the cave during the day as if they were lost.

Several times in the next few weeks we heard the sound of baying dogs off in the distance from different directions, and then the forest seemed to return to normal. At night, as we talked around our campfire, we discussed our alternatives.

"If we stay out of their way long enough, they may grow tired of looking for us and leave us alone," one of the half-castes said.

"We need to make a stand against them," someone else said. "Otherwise they will just pick us off one at a time."

"That's just crazy talk, we don't even know how many of 'us' there are any more. What kind of an army would we make?"

"We didn't think we had a chance against Feardorcha either but we sure surprised everyone didn't we?" said Mathuin.

"Maybe we should just try to smuggle each of us out of the country one by one," someone else offered.

"Oh, so you think we would be so much more welcome in another country?" someone said.

"I don't want to leave. This is my home. We have as much right here as anyone else," said Honora. "Somewhere else we would be half-castes and foreigners to boot."

"We're forgetting that we really do have a reason to be here," said Wilo. "They need us here. There are things we can do that they can't do, unless we teach them. We have to think of a way to show them how much they need us. We have to try to think like them."

"What is it they value?" Wilo mused.

"They value money," I said. "It was money that brought the hunters in after us. They were each promised a fortune if they were successful".

"Yes, money motivates many men, but not Varley."

"It would seem that revenge motivates him," said my father, "but maybe you could say that love motivates him in a way. I understand Varley's desire for vengeance in the face of his loss. But what fuels it now? Why hasn't he sickened of it? What makes him different from me? I think it has to be that he has no hope. No hope for happiness with the woman he loved, no hope for forgiveness, no hope for a world he can control."

"Let me get this right," said a confused listener. "We're supposed to be giving hope to the man who's trying to kill us?"

"Hope and a new viewpoint," said Wilo. "But we can't expect him to listen to us just because we want him to. We're going to have to convince him he wants to talk to us first. He's got to have a reason to want to."

A mouse that had been snuggled up next to a faerie child, spoke up, "I know what might convince him."

"What's that, Tiptoe?" Fiona asked.

"In his dreams he begs for Oona's forgiveness. Then when he wakes in the morning he has forgotten, or he's too ashamed to admit it. At least that's what we used to think. My family, that is. We used to live in the cupboard of his private chamber. I haven't always been a country mouse you know."

"How is it that you've never mentioned that before?" asked Wilo.

"Well we were run out of there, you know. Not the most glorious chapter of our family history. I lost seven members of my family between the traps and the cat."

"Sorry Tiptoe. Thank you for the information."

"This is very interesting indeed," said Raemann. "I had no idea the man had any such sensibilities."

"Yes," said my father, "we do tend to see our enemies as one dimensional. We have to demonize them in order to give ourselves permission to hate them instead of seeing them for what they are, flawed and fallible just like us."

"I don't need permission to hate him. He's given me plenty of reasons for that," said a veteran refugee.

"Yes, we all have reasons to hate Varley, but we're trying to understand him. Maybe that's the only way out of this trap that has become our lives," said Raemann.

"Wait a minute, you can't trust a man like Varley. He's shown his true colors time and time again," said the veteran.

"And right now he's saying something similar about faerie folk and mixed bloods. When will it ever end?" This was spoken by me with a gesture of frustration.

"OK," said Wilo, trying to get us back on track, "what is the best way we can use this information?"

"Maybe we can ask Oona to visit him. Maybe she could bring Lord Varley's wife with her. That is, if they've met up," said an old woman.

"Hello, last time I noticed, Oona wasn't doing house calls. She isn't exactly at our beck and call."

"Maybe not, but we do have a pretty influential group here, including her husband and her son. She did call us her children too," said a woman who had been at Oona's Yew the night of Feardorcha's disgrace.

"Oona, you have come to our aid before. Can you help us now, in the Creator's name?" asked Honora for all of us.

There was no response, no green glow, no mellifluous voice. Just silence. We hadn't really expected a response, just kind of hoped for one.

CHAPTER 17

BLACK WATERS

Feardorcha had disappeared after his humiliation at Oona's Yew. The public was starting to breathe easy, hoping he was gone for good. Such was far from the case. Feardorcha had taken refuge on Brennan's Island, as Wilo had named it. There he was setting up his offensive, away from prying eyes. Meanwhile his spies were everywhere on the mainland, most especially scouring the waterfront from any vantage point that might be possible to launch a small boat. The main ports had become much too dangerous to make an escape from. Varley's soldiers patrolled them day and night. Cliffs, shoals, and treacherous currents made remote areas too dangerous in other ways. But there were numerous private beaches where a small craft could launch successfully. It was to one of these that Wilo had directed Wolf and his gang. Thinking the island was deserted, she had unknowingly sent them directly into his reach! As related to us later, they had parted from the gypsies and had traveled many long miles on foot to reach their destination. They had seen no one along the way. The cottage they had expected to find looked deserted. A garden planted that spring with herbs and vegetables was overgrown with weeds and vines. The couple that Wilo had known and sent them to, had been captured and were no longer there. As they approached the door of the cottage they were greeted by the smell of onions frying. A short bald man with a pleasant ruddy face greeted them at the door.

"Anything I can help you young people with?" he asked.

"We were hoping to buy a boat from you," Wolf said.

"Well now, boats are a precious commodity around these parts, especially lately. What makes you think you can afford to buy my boat?" said the short man.

Wolf and his mates looked at each other, unsure what to say next.

"We were told by a friend that you might have one for sale," said Wolf, a bit unsteadily.

"Oh, and who might that friend be?" asked the short man.

"Wilo told us," a girl offered.

"Wilo, you say. Well then, why don't you come on in and make yourselves comfortable. You must be tired after your long journey. And hungry too, I would imagine."

He excused himself and went around back to a pigeon coop where he scribbled a note and attached the note to a pigeon's leg and sent it flying. Then he returned with some more onions and some pigeon eggs to fry up for his guests.

"I hope you won't mind putting up with my hospitality for a couple of days," their host said pleasantly. "You see the decision isn't entirely up to me, and my wife won't be back for a little while. Just a couple of days, you understand. She's off to visit her sister. We'll need her permission as well. I can make you comfortable here until then."

"We don't mind," a couple of the girls said happily, thinking how wonderful a good night's sleep in a real bed would feel in the relative safety of this secluded cottage.

"All right then, it's agreed. I don't get many visitors. It will be nice to have someone to talk to. Would you like something to drink? I have a barrel of some very good ale in the cellar. Let me get you some. Then you can tell me all about what's going on in the rest of the world.

Feardorcha received the message by pigeon late the next day. The message he sent in return said only this; "Send them to me."

Meanwhile, Varley himself, his sleep troubled by unsettling dreams of his past sins and his own demise, had sent to have a gypsy fortune teller brought to him. The old woman had a reputation for her predictions which caused her to be held in awe by many of the townspeople and some of the soldiers as well. Varley hoped to use her to gain some advantage in his war against the outcasts. But more that that, he wished to know the time and manner of his own death, and who would be responsible for it. He hoped knowing this, would allow him to have that person eliminated, and return to him the gift of sleep; one of the few gifts that can't be bought, and which is valued best, like most gifts, when it is no longer there.

Varley had the old woman brought to a tower room in his fortress and posted guards outside the door. He wanted no one to be witness to what she was to tell him there.

"Old woman, I understand that you are able to foretell the future, is this so?" he asked.

"You don't need me to tell you what your future will bring. Your past has done that for you," she responded. "Your dreams haven't given you a clue?"

"What do you know of my dreams?" said Varley, somewhat alarmed.

"I only know what you tell me, by your words and by your actions. I can see that you haven't slept for many nights. If your sleep is troubled by dreams then the dreams may hold a clue."

He considered this, and his attitude underwent a change.

"Can a person change his fate?" he asked her earnestly. "Can what has been foretold be changed?"

"That depends on your intent," She responded.

"The intent is to change the outcome!" he said impatiently.

She didn't respond to this, and Varley stood over her threateningly. She gazed back at him calmly. "Do you wish me to read your palm?" she asked.

"Palm, crystal ball, tea leaves, whatever it is that you do, let's get on with it," he said.

She took a small crystal ball, about the size of an orange, from a leather pouch that hung from her waist. She placed it on the table in front of her and motioned for him to sit across from her.

"I see all the deeds of your past coming together to pull you down below black waters."

"Yes, in my dreams something is pulling me down. I'm trying to gasp for air and the weight is pulling me under the surface. That's how she died, you know. She drowned trying to escape from one of those unnatural creatures. Oh, my beautiful Siobhan!"

Tears welled in his eyes as he described her thus and he squeezed the lids tight shut to stop the tears from falling. Then the fearsome Varley was back again wanting control, and he pounded the table with his fist.

"Can you see anyone, can you see who it is that is trying to drown me?" he asked.

"I see no man," she said. "I see only a woman. A beautiful woman. Walking in a garden by a stream. It's very peaceful."

"Is her hair golden and are her eyes green? Is she tall and slender?" he asked.

"She is as you say," responded the gypsy.

"That is Siobhan!" he cried. "She loved the garden."

"If this is my future, then Siobhan is in my future?" he asked.

"The choice is yours; with Siobhan in the garden, or the black waters."

"Well then the choice is simple," said Varley, laughing.

"As I said," the gypsy responded, "It all depends upon your intent."

"Can you tell me nothing further about who it is that intends to drown me?" he asked.

"It is no man," she replied again. "Look to yourself, Varley. The weight that pulls you down is of your own making."

"Can you see nothing else?" he asked.

"Your Lady is joined by a companion," said the gypsy. "It's Oona, the Lady of the Yew Tree," she continued, "they are walking arm in arm."

"She has befriended Siobhan?" he asked.

"It would appear so," said the old woman.

"Then perhaps there is hope that I can be forgiven," he said, almost under his breath.

"There is always hope," said the old woman. "While there is breath there is hope."

Varley seemed pleased with the information the old gypsy woman had provided him. He had her escorted back to her camp with the admonition that he would be sending for her again and would expect her compliance. When next we met with the gypsies and they were able to pass this information on to us, we were overjoyed at the fortuitous turn of events. It gave us access to Varley's frame of mind and possibly an opportunity to influence it. It was also evident that he didn't suspect a connection between the gypsies and the outcasts, and this was good news as well. The gypsies told us of their parting from Wolf's group and we hoped that they had gotten to the island without more trouble. Cailean expected her hawk to return at any time with some word of their safe arrival.

Meanwhile, back at the cave, an unexpected turn of events had given us cause for celebration and for sadness. It seems a certain hunter with markedly crooked teeth had fallen into a bear trap set by another group of hunters and been impaled, along with two of his dogs, on the sharp stakes planted upright at the bottom of the trap. The others had managed to avoid it. When his companions carried him away they left his cap behind; a cap with a fox's tail for trim. It was borne back to the cave by a raven that witnessed the event and described it in detail.

The death of the hunter marked a short period of relative calm for the outcasts. It also proved without a doubt what we had all been fearing; that the mother fox would not be coming home. We buried the hat since we had no more left of her to honor, that and the memory of a brave and devoted mother and friend. The young foxes were nearly grown now, and since their mother had taught them well, they would be able to take care of themselves. Fiona had bonded strongly with them and identified with them completely, having lost a mother herself. In some ways they looked to her as a surrogate mother. When stories were told around the campfire, as they often were, Fiona always included the story of the brave fox mother who risked her own life so that her children and her friends would be spared. Flit, Finn, Flann, and Flossy would listen gravely but proudly, and there was never a dry eye in the crowd. She would live on in all of our memories to inspire us and our children as long as stories are told, just as I am telling you now.

CHAPTER 18

THE SILKEN LAIR

Wolf's pack made it to the island safely with Cailean's hawk as guide, but they were not to be masters of the island as they expected. As they approached the island they could see the tents and banners of what looked to be a carnival in progress. They were met at the beach with much pomp and circumstance, and brought to the lighthouse tower, where Feardorcha had set up his headquarters. He eyed them now with the assurance of a well-fed spider surveying his next meal. There was no hurry. He would get what he wanted eventually. He could play with them a while, reel them deeper into the web. He was bored with the company on the island and they were a welcome diversion. He was kind to them. They were offered food, the like of which they hadn't tasted in all of their young lives. They were given fresh clothing of the softest fabrics, much finer than they had ever seen. They were shown to a large tent made comfortable with silk cushions in glorious colors, and told to rest from the ardors of their journey. Later, Feardorcha said, they would talk.

The teenagers, while duly impressed, were not unaware of the danger they were in. Their young lives had been shaped by the fear that the dual threat of Feardorcha and Lord Varley posed for their families. They were plucky and resilient, but their trademark overconfidence had taken a beating. What could the six of them hope to do to secure their futures, now that Feardorcha was no longer a distant threat, but their host, and in reality, their captor? They discussed this now in hushed tones.

"Don't get too comfortable there grunions, you know he's just playing us," said Wolf.

"Of course he is," said Sena, the most outspoken girl. "There's no saying we can't play him a bit too, is there? We can pretend we're going along with him. We don't have a lot of choices really, but that's one."

"One thing is certain, unless we are very careful, he will know everything we say just as soon as it is out of our mouths," said Ginger, a large girl with a broad, pleasant face.

"I checked outside the tent, there is no one within thirty yards of it," said Wolf's second in command, Biskit, a tall whippet thin lad.

"That's well and good for now, but don't let any of us forget to keep up our guard," said Wolf, "no matter how comfortable he makes us feel."

Feardorcha was again the model host at their next meeting. His questions were all about their comfort, their needs and desires.

Sena's friend Dorcas obliged him by asking for a persimmon. "I've heard of them," she said, "and I've always wanted to try one."

Feardorcha gave her the most ingratiating of smiles and said, "I think that can be arranged."

When they returned to their tent, a large bowl featuring persimmons, dates, plums, figs, nuts and a pineapple was awaiting them in their tent. The others all turned to Dorcas the minute they were inside.

"Dorcas, you are such a ninny. We don't ask favors of Feardorcha. He is not someone you want to be indebted to," said Fergus, a boy of medium build and nervous demeanor.

"Well you are all eating his food too, I was just being polite and making conversation," she said, her pride wounded.

"That is just the kind of thing I was referring to," said Wolf. "You let your guard down and before you know it you will be making polite conversation about the people back at the cave. Do not forget for one minute that we are his prisoners."

Dorcas knew he was right, and she was feeling apologetic. "I'm sorry Wolf, I'm just not used to playing this game. I'm used to saying what I think."

"You never think," said Sena, "you just say whatever pops into your head."

"If we want to get out of this alive without betraying the others we're going to have to consider the consequences of our actions and our words and keep our wits about us at all times," said Wolf. "Other people are depending on us."

"I can't believe you just said that, Wolf, you sound just like Raemann," said Sena.

"I'm beginning to understand him," said Wolf.

The next time they were called in to Feardorcha's presence he was concerned for the welfare of those they had left behind. He enquired about their families, and the state of their health, after so long in hiding. Wolf was not about to be so easily tricked into admitting anything that would implicate their families.

"You make an assumption there," Wolf said. "Our families weren't in hiding, only us. We had disagreements with them and left on our own."

"Is that so?" Feardorcha said, "how unfortunate."

"And what of this person Wilo, who supplied you with the information to make your way to this island. You still think of her as a friend, do you?"

The friends looked from one to the other for a response, not knowing what to think or say. Doubt had been planted in their minds with that one harmless sentence.

"Surely you can tell me something about her," Feardorcha said, "She seems remarkable in every way." Then Feardorcha addressed Dorcas, "What is your opinion of this Wilo, Miss Dorcas?"

Dorcas was biting her lip and looking at the patterns of the carpet at her feet. "She's all right I guess, a bit bossy though," she replied, her eyes still on the carpet.

"Is that so?" Feardorcha commiserated. "Still I think I should like to meet her." He clapped his hands together and two servants appeared, a stubby grizzled pair of curiosities whose homely features suffered in comparison to their resplendently garish scarlet and yellow satin garments.

"We are at your service master," they said, bowing low while their beady eyes nervously scanned the perimeter of the room.

"Make sure that our young guests have everything they need. I put you in charge of their well-being. I'm sure you know how to make them comfortable."

The hawk finally returned to tell us about the misfortune that had befallen Wolf's hapless group of young people. At least we knew, for the time being, that they hadn't been harmed. We considered our alternatives.

"I don't know how long they can hold out against Feardorcha. He's bound to find out from them where to find us."

"It seems to me," said Wilo, "that the best course of action is the most unlikely one. Varley is our best bet right now. He has given us an opening and we have to pursue it as an option."

Cailean returned to the gypsy camp to advise the old gypsy woman and the others of the situation. She was happy to help us as long as we understood that she would only be telling Varley exactly what she saw in the crystal ball.

"I only tell him what I see. What he does with it is up to him. Usually people want me to tell them what it means. What I tell them is only the most obvious alternative and they are free not to choose it or to interpret it differently."

When next Varley sent for the old gypsy, he appeared to be in a highly agitated state. He had been much encouraged by a dream he'd had the previous night, in which his beloved Siobhan appeared walking side by side with Oona in the garden. In the dream they were walking away from him and then Siobhan turned and beckoned to him to join them. She smiled her lovely smile as if to encourage him. He wanted to follow them but something held him back. He thought; "If only Oona would turn and smile at me I would know I am forgiven and I would gladly follow." But Oona only paused and looked out over the fields of flowers and then both women turned and resumed their walk without looking back again.

"What does the dream mean?" he asked. "Have my fortunes changed for the better?"

The gypsy took out her crystal ball and gazed intently into its depths. After some time Varley's patience began to wane and his curiosity got the better of him. He began to question her. Knowing full well that she would answer when she was ready and not before, still he hoped to move the process along to its fulfillment more quickly.

It's difficult for men like Varley to be patient; they are used to having their wishes and commands met immediately. It's also one of the reasons why they find life so difficult to enjoy. Many of the greatest pleasures of life can only be enjoyed after years of effort have been put in first. The difficult work must be put in personally not substituted by someone else.

Finally the gypsy answered: "There is another that has joined the two in the garden."

"Who is it?" Varley asked. "Describe them to me."

"It is a mort-sidhe child, a male, that wears the colors and emblem of the house of Varley," said the gypsy, looking intently at the man who stood before her. Her fate and that of many others, he held in his hands.

"What do they ask of me?" was his response.

"Your crusade against those of mixed blood has left many orphans," said the gypsy.

"To prove that you are truly sorry, Oona and Siobhan ask that you adopt one of the orphans that you created and raise him as your own son."

"More than anything else in this life I wish to be forgiven by Oona and reunited with Siobhan. I would pay any price, shoulder any burden. But I do not know If I can do this thing they ask," was his reply.

"Then truly your fate is in your own hands," the gypsy responded, and she stood up and turned to leave the room.

"And if I should take up this challenge, who is to decide if I have done a satisfactory job?" Varley asked.

"Let your conscience be your guide, and if you have doubts, Oona and Siobhan will set you on the right path. I will bring a suitable child to you. Under no circumstances is he to be harmed in any way. I need not tell you that your immortal soul, and everything you hold dear, depend upon it."

CHAPTER 19

THE ORPHAN

Another summer had gone to seed, the few remaining days clinging to the seed head until they flew, one by one with the north wind, to that place that all summers go to await the spring. The cave dwellers dreaded the thought of winter. Our footsteps would be easy to track in the snow, and while our efforts to put away enough supplies for those bitter months were prodigious, we weren't at all sure they were sufficient to our needs. Because we feared a winter without enough provisions, and because the soldier's patrols of the forest had become infrequent, we had relaxed our rule of having only two of us above ground at one time.

Flit and Fiona were sometimes joined by Flossy on their excursions, but Finn and Flann were seen increasingly less often, and had staked out new territories for themselves, as foxes will. The area in immediate proximity to the cave was left untouched so as to not give indication of our whereabouts, and the area we determined to be a safe distance away had long ago been scoured of berries, roots, tubers, herbs, and dry wood. Provisioning trips were now a several day affair.

Flit and Fiona headed off along the river toward the coast with the intention of catching and drying fish for our larder. They had found a stream where they were having quite a bit of success catching salmon, which were running at this time of year, and drying them on racks above the narrow beach. Flit would catch the fish and toss them on the beach, where Fiona retrieved them and filleted them. After several days' effort they were taking a much deserved rest, in the shade of some willows, where they could watch for any creatures passing by that might try to make off with their catch.

"Very well done Flit, you are such a good fisherman! I don't think anyone, even Matt or Brennan, could have done as well. Everyone will be so pleased with us when they see what we have to contribute."

Flit lay with his head on his neat black paws, panting happily. His handsome red coat was nearly dry and he rolled over on his back and moved all four legs in the air as if he were trotting, and looked over at Fiona with a grin on his pointy muzzle. Fiona laughed at him.

"Yes, it would be nice if we could both travel on the air like that to get the fish back to the cave, but I can only fly when I am small, and even if I concentrated as hard as I could I'd only be able to move you and the fish a few feet. So my friend, we will have to be beasts of burden."

While they were thus engaged in conversation, a party of travelers following the river down from the coast, happened upon the drying salmon and called out for the owners to come forward, so that they might barter for a share of it. Flit and Fiona noticed the familiar faces of Wolf's group of teenagers among the party, but they were wary enough of the others to remain where they were in hiding.

"Is this the work of your friends do you suppose?" asked the man who appeared to be leading the group.

"I told you," Wolf responded, "they aren't our friends. We don't have any reason to be protecting them. They kicked us out."

"Yes, so you say. They kicked you out and yet gave you instructions as to how you might get to the island safely."

"My point exactly," said Wolf. "They weren't doing us any favors, obviously. They probably knew you were waiting for us there."

"Then you won't have any issues of conscience in returning the favor."

"Absolutely not. That is my intention entirely," Wolf responded.

"How far are we from their main camp?" asked the leader of the expedition.

"Not far now," Wolf replied, "but like I said, they move around a lot. I can't say where they will be for sure. If we wait here we will probably catch some of them when they come back for their fish."

"You are not telling me anything that I haven't already figured out for myself," the leader growled.

"Well, I can show you some more places they are likely to be if you prefer," Wolf responded.

"Indeed you will, and I will post a guard here as well," the leader said.

The group moved on then, helping themselves to some of the fish, and leaving two of their number behind to watch the rest. A miniaturized Fiona snuggled into Flit's neck fur and they disappeared into the forest leaving their hard won provisions behind. They needed to make it back to the cave with a warning about the approaching peril.

The old Gypsy woman had found an orphan she considered suitable as a foster child for Lord Varley. There were many orphans to choose from, but this one needed to possess exceptional qualities unique to the situation. The old woman considered the abilities and needs of the child, as well as the needs and personality of Lord Varley, in making her choice. Her selection was a precocious eight year old named Solomon and nicknamed Sol. His large dark eyes sparkled with intelligence and wit, but a solemn reticence gave him the unnerving quality of a much older and wiser spirit within.

Sol had been an orphan since the age of three and he vaguely remembered a family and happier times. Since the death of his parents he had been shuffled from one distant family member to another. Times being as they were, there was never enough to go around, so Solomon became one of the youngest members at the Academy. It was the same Solomon who had so idolized Mathuin and imitated him to our amusement. When the Gypsy came enquiring after orphans, she heard from many sources of this exceptional child, whom many felt deserved the opportunity, and was equally up to the challenge it presented.

Sol's pedigree would have impressed anyone less rabid about the mixing of bloods, as he could claim royalty among both his mother's faerie side, and somewhat more distantly on his father's side. Though the blessings of a human sacrament would never have been allowed by his father's people, a faerie ceremony had legitimized the union among all who knew the couple and understood these matters of the heart.

As to the child, he had been told that he was being adopted by a man of great influence, who was childless, and had lost his beloved wife. The child's own losses predisposed him to empathy, and his contemplative nature inclined him toward patience; not normally demonstrated by one so young. As I have already indicated, Lord Varley himself was not a patient man, but he did pride himself in being able to recognize sterling qualities in those he surrounded himself with, and rewarding them. After all, he had wooed and won Siobhan, when he was as yet an undistinguished soldier. His fiefdom was a reward for loyalty and bravery in the service of his king.

Varley had arranged for a host of nannies and educators to serve as surrogate parents, and hoped to defer his responsibility in the rearing of the child in this manner. He intended to spend as little time with the boy as he deemed necessary. In truth, he didn't trust himself to do an adequate job of parenting any child, let alone one of mixed blood, but he didn't want to fail Siobhan, and he took Oona's challenge seriously. It might have been different, he thought, if Siobhan were still alive. He remembered how much she had longed for a child of their own to raise.

At the appointed time, the old Gypsy arrived, with the child in hand, and presented him to Lord Varley. Varley received them somewhat coolly, and was about to hand the boy off to a nanny, when he noticed the boy's gaze struck upon the full length portrait of Siobhan that graced the great hall.

"That is your lady that you grieve for," said the boy, looking up at the man and then returning his gaze to the portrait. "I wish I could have known her. She looks very kind and beautiful."

The nanny led him away to his new quarters, and Varley watched his straight little back as he walked away, as if he were taking his measure. The Gypsy woman was likewise watching Varley.

"He is an exceptional boy, but he is yet a child and has a child's needs for affection as well as education," said the old woman. "I see you have provided for the training, that is a start, and maybe not such a bad one."

That said, the old woman left the man and child to work out the details of their relationship.

CHAPTER 20

THE CAPTIVE

Mathuin and I had been working hard at reducing felled trees to logs that we could carry back to the cave for our winter store of firewood. Mathuin had spotted an ancient cherry tree with a burled and twisted trunk that had come down in the last storm. He thought the wood could be worked into a beautiful box to hold the shells and other adornments that Wilo liked to fasten into her hair. That was his intention on this particular day. I had an idea of my own, for a surprise for Cailean, so after I had helped him chop the venerable tree into manageable chunks, we parted company. I headed out along the river in search of the smooth banded stones that Cailean liked so well. I wanted a few more prime examples to fashion into a necklace for her. I had been practicing with a metal worker among our group of fugitives, and felt confident that I could make something that would delight her.

I will admit that I was not particularly wary at that point, being lost in my thoughts of Cailean. Luckily my ability to slip into hyper-awareness was beginning to be almost unconsciously conditioned by what was going on around me. Sometimes I had to purposely try to tune it out so that I could concentrate on a task at hand. One second my thoughts were indulgently on Cailean, and then in a split second I was aware of something not being right in the atmosphere around me and every nerve ending was on alert. I slipped into the hollow of a lightning-struck tree and took stock of the situation. The animals had ceased their chattering and were quiet except for the warning cry of a bird from overhead. I knew that there were people, and danger, just out of range of my sight. I said a quiet prayer for those I knew to be out of the cave that day, including Mathuin, who had to trust to their human senses. As silently as possible I crept to the top of a rise that looked down over the glen where I sensed the danger to be; the glen where I had left Mathuin intent on carving something beautiful for Wilo.

What I saw was this; Wolf and his group approaching Mathuin, him standing up and coming toward them to greet them, and from all around them men coming to attack Mathuin, striking him, securing his arms behind him as he struggled, hitting and kicking him until he lay still on the ground at their feet. When he stirred they forced him to his knees and interrogated him. He said not a word even with a knife at his throat.

"Don't kill him," said Dorcas, "that's Wilo's sweetheart. It's her you want isn't it? He's your best bet for catching her." Mathuin threw her a sharp look.

"Well what do you know, looks like we hit the jackpot today," said one of the men. "Feardorcha will be pleased."

They forced Mathuin to his feet and led him away with them. I noticed that Wolf was leading them away from the cave. When they were out of sight I retrieved the unfinished box that Mathuin had roughed out of the cherry wood and carried it with me back to the cave to let the others know what had happened.

Wilo was grave but calm. "How many men were there?" she wanted to know.

When I told her there were thirty or more she only nodded. I explained what Dorcas had said and how it affected the captors. I told them how Wolf had led them away from the cave and that I thought we could feel that Mathuin wasn't alone even if they had to pretend to be his enemies. I gave Wilo the box and told her that Mathuin had been making it for her. She took the box and went off by herself. She clutched the box to her heart and sobbed. None of us knew what to do. None of us had seen Wilo like this before. Wilo remained silent while the rest of us talked quietly about what we should do. No one had seen Flit and Fiona for a couple of days and we were worried about them as well. That night none of us slept very well.

I wasn't asleep, but staring up through my window to the stars and thinking what to do, when Wilo found me in my alcove under the tree roots.

"I'm going to get him back," she whispered.

"What do you want to do, Wilo? I'll do anything to help you get Mathuin back if we can only think of something that might work."

"I knew you would Brennan. I have a plan, I don't know if there is much chance of it working, but we have to try. Are you with me anyway?"

"I love Mathuin too Wilo, I couldn't live with myself if we didn't do something. What is your plan?"

"I am going to offer myself as ransom," said Wilo.

"What do you mean, Wilo, you can't do that! What possible purpose could it serve?"

"You told me yourself that it was me they wanted," said Wilo. "I'm not going to let them torture him to find me. Besides, that's just my part of this. Your part comes next."

"All right Wilo, tell me what your plan is," I said.

"The Wizard of Oona's Yew is going to challenge Feardorcha again. This time he will offer me as ransom if he loses, and we get Mathuin if Feardorcha loses."

"I see only one problem with that plan, Wilo," I said. "I can't win against Feardorcha! I don't have that kind of power!"

"You have more power than you know, Brennan. And besides, you won't be alone in this. This is our moment, Brennan, the time we have been preparing for. We must call on all our support and all our resources for this final showdown. You have to have faith in me Brennan, and we have to have faith in our cause, that it is just and that it is necessary, regardless of the outcome. If you have that faith, then the others will follow you. Remember, you are Oona's son."

I thought of my mother then, and how she had come to our aid the last time the wizard had appeared. I pictured in my mind what the old gypsy woman had told us of Varley's dreams; how Oona and Siobhan walked together in the garden.

"What news is there of Varley and the orphan he took in?" I asked her.

"Cailean is expected back from the gypsy camp tomorrow. She would have the most recent knowledge," Wilo replied.

"I've been thinking of Varley too," said Wilo. "With Varley and Feardorcha together we don't stand much of a chance. If Varley sits this battle out it really is in his best interest. He doesn't want to displease Siobhan and Oona, but he hasn't changed his colors that much. If he waits to see what the outcome is, he can't be held responsible if it doesn't go well for us."

"Yes, I think that's how he would see it," I responded. "Our main concern is Feardorcha.

Even still, we were so lucky last time," I said. "It's expecting a lot to think we could be that lucky again."

"Don't you see Brennan, it isn't luck!" Said Wilo, her eyes glowing with certainty. "Whatever happens is created out of the faith that we hold in what is right!"

"Then we had better not lose faith or it will be 'might makes right' as it seems to have so many times in the past," I said.

Wilo was standing now, looking out the window to the moon. She was quiet for a very long time, long enough so that I had time to regret what I had said, but not long enough for me to think up something to say to make it better. Finally she spoke.

"I know you have doubts, Brennan. How could you not, with a history like yours. We are mortal, and we all have doubts about whether our lives have meaning and purpose or are just sands in an hourglass. There are many things beyond our knowing, but we ultimately determine what meaning our lives have by the choices we make. Varley has chosen vengeance to shape his life. He is beginning to see the folly of that, whether or not he can see his way clear to change, is yet to be seen. Feardorcha has chosen power to shape his. It would seem that power is vastly superior to anything that we puny outcasts could have chosen to shape our lives. Do you really believe that is so, Brennan? What is it that you stand for? What have you chosen to shape the meaning of your life?"

I had never really thought about it before, and I thought about it now. My life, since I had awakened less than two years ago, seemed like a series of reactions to the events that were swirling around me. My friends were central to its meaning, I knew that without them life would have little meaning for me. Anything that threatened them was something I knew I could stand against. That I could do, and the outcome was out of my hands; leave that to the historians to figure out. I stood for my friends, and for the lives of peace and contentment that we all deserved and longed for, no more or less than any man.

Flit and Fiona had watched from a distance while Feardorcha's men stuffed their packsacks with the fish that the fox and faerie child had caught and dried. When the men, led by Wolf's group, had set off downstream, the youngsters had followed them at a safe distance and had witnessed Mathuin's capture. They had observed my return to the cave, and knew the others had been informed. They had decided their best move was to follow Mathuin and make note of where he was being held. They discovered that the group that had captured Mathuin, was just the vanguard of a large encampment at the edge of the forest. Feardorcha's tent was at the center of that encampment. It was there that Mathuin had been brought.

Flit and Fiona had been gone a long time. Everyone at the cave was relieved when they finally showed up footsore and out of breath. Fiona stumbled over her words in her haste to explain to us what she and Flit had observed. Raemann and Honora and the others crowded around them with questions about Mathuin's condition and details about where he was being held.

A subdued welcome was planned for Cailean; she was expected anytime now, but with conditions in the countryside such as they were, we were all worried about her. She knew immediately, upon arriving, that something was wrong, and her joyful expression dissolved in apprehension. She looked around at all of our faces, then not finding Mathuin's among them she insisted; "Where is Mathuin? Is he coming later?" The answer was beginning to dawn on her but her heart rejected it. "Brennan, where is Mathuin?" she implored me. I wrapped her up in my arms and held her close.

"He's been captured, Cailean, but we're going to get him back," I said, trying to console her, but meaning it too.

"We have a plan, but it needs more work," said Wilo. "We will get him back."

Long into the night the cave dwellers crowded around the fire talking of our love for Mathuin, recounting the stories that each of us carried around with us, many which we had never told before; of some special way that he had inspired or protected us or made us laugh. Mathuin was a quiet person, not inclined to putting forth his opinions, usually taking a position toward the back of the room in our discussions, letting the more vocal members of the group have their say and engage in the usual debates or even heated arguments that would develop. As we told our stories of Mathuin, it became evident that to each of us, some small kindness, or true words spoken, had been treasured by each of us and carried within us as a talisman to guide us and give us strength. As we spoke, the somber, weighted atmosphere of the cave dissipated, and our love and resolve seemed to multiply. I looked around me at the circle of earnest faces. The fire glowed brightly, and lit up each face, even as their forms melted into the shadows in the room. I saw those faces and the faces of multitudes of others transported to the forest just outside of Feardorcha's encampment. I saw the lights of faerie illuminating the faces, and heard the roar, and shrieks, and hisses, of the animals. Yes, we were a fearsome lot indeed. A force of nature, and the most powerful force of all, the force of love. Nothing is fiercer than that when it is threatened. I no longer doubted the way we must go, or my role in it, but was filled with a peace and calm that seemed to radiate from within.

"Mother we are ready," I said, as the group grew quiet and thoughtful. "We know our purpose and we are ready."

CHAPTER 21

KINDRED SPIRITS

Flit and Fiona hadn't seen the other young foxes for several weeks. The day held the promise of sunshine and mild weather, perhaps one of the last such days before the dread of a long cold winter. To make the best use of it, the youngsters decided to embark on a search to look up the fox siblings. Flit seemed to have some ideas about where they might be. They packed some provisions and headed out early before the others at the cave were awake.

They found Flossy first. She had found a mate for herself, a young male that had been born the previous spring, to a vixen that had been a friend of Flossy's mother. They had chosen a location for a den, their first litter of kits would be born in early spring. Flossy was overjoyed to see them, and share her happiness with them. Finn and Flann had last been seen by Flossy traveling together but that was a week or so earlier.

After an exchange of news, about goings on at the cave, and a retelling of the capture of Mathuin, Flit and

Fiona continued on their search for the two brothers. They found them in a meadow of tall, dried grasses, by turns leaping up above the grass to pounce on a rodent or grasshopper, and then disappearing again behind a waving wall of flax. Flit and Fiona decided to sneak up on them. Fiona miniaturized, and they stayed low in the grass, and followed the curve of an ancient stone foundation until they were almost on top of them. At the end of the foundation, where the last stone trailed into the meadow, they were surprised by a sudden movement. A boy with large dark eyes, had been equally surprised by their approach, and jumped up from where he had been hidden in the grass watching the antics of the fox brothers. He looked startled for a moment, then his body relaxed into an observant stance, as the fox and boy took stock of each other. Flann and Finn had stopped their bouncing and were stealthily approaching the pair through the grass. Fiona had not yet made herself known. She decided to speak;

"Who are you, and what is your purpose here?" she asked.

The boy took the apparently talking fox in his stride.

"I am Solomon and I have come on a walk to survey my father's lands. I happened upon these two very funny fellows. I didn't want to scare them away because I was enjoying watching them. I didn't mean to harm them."

Deciding that the boy was truthful, Fiona resumed her normal size. "You are right, they are very funny fellows. Flit and I usually find them amusing. Their names are Finn and Flann. I am Fiona."

The boy took off his cap and bowed to them, saying, "I am most pleased to make your acquaintance."

"You have very nice manners," said Fiona, "but how is it that I have never seen you before? We know these parts very well."

"I am just newly moved here," the boy responded. "I have been adopted by the Lord of this land."

"Then I have heard of you," said Fiona. "And how are you being treated there?"

"Well," the boy responded, "I don't actually see my father much, but I do feel he is trying his best to be a good father. He has provided me with everything I could possibly want. I, in turn, am trying to be a good son. I am trying very hard to learn everything he wishes me to know. Sometimes I wish he would just walk with me. We could have enjoyed watching Finn and Flann together."

"Your father would probably prefer watching the foxes from the back of a horse with a pack of baying hounds," said Fiona.

The boy looked stung by that comment, but he didn't protest it. "I know that many people don't like my father," said the boy, "but they don't see him as I do. He does have feelings. There are many things he worries about. His dreams trouble him. He is sorry for many of the people he has hurt. You may not know that he has begun paying restitution to the families he has wronged."

"I don't know if even Lord Varley has enough resources for that," Fiona responded, tucking the information away in her memory where it would be retrieved later and relayed to the cave dwellers.

"What sort of things is your father interested in having you learn?" Fiona asked.

"Languages, figures, astronomy, he's very keen on history and bridge building."

"With all that to learn, I'm surprised you are allowed to be wandering the fields alone," said Fiona.

"Well I'm not really alone, exactly. The governess took me on a nature walk. The observance of nature is one of my lessons for today. She knows all of the useful herbs and the names of most of the birds and insects. We were to sketch them and label them to show father later. She had to meet someone and asked me to stay put and draw while she was gone. I think she has a boyfriend. She will be back soon, she's never gone for very long."

He showed us his sketchbook then, with clever sketches of flowers and plants, butterflies and caterpillars. The last sketch, not quite done, was of a comical Finn and Flann leaping above the grass, eyes intent on their prey and unaware of the quiet boy with the sketchbook observing their every move.

"These are very good," said Fiona, with admiration. "You have certainly captured the essence of Finn and Flann, right down to the daffy, eager expression on Flann's face."

Flann looked at the sketch and smiled, with his head to the side and his tongue lolling out the side of his mouth. He was still panting from the exertion of his leaping.

"Maybe it would be best if we weren't here when your governess comes back," said Fiona.

"Maybe so," said Solomon, "but I'd like to see you again." He rarely saw anyone his own age and really didn't want to say goodbye.

"We always take our nature walks on Tuesday mornings, unless it's raining. Will I see you again?"

"Yes, Solomon, I promise," said Fiona, who felt she had found a kindred spirit in the quiet boy who saw her foxes just as she did.

"We'll be back next Tuesday morning," said Fiona.

"Unless it's raining," said Solomon.

"Unless it's raining," agreed Fiona.

Later, when they had returned to the cave, Fiona related to the others her meeting with Lord Varley's young charge. "We met Solomon," said Fiona. "He made this drawing of Finn and Flann. Isn't he really good? Solomon said that Lord Varley has been paying restitution to the families he has harmed."

"Maybe that means he is no longer rounding up the mort-sidhe. Maybe we can come out of hiding," said one of the cave dwellers.

"While this is hopeful news, we must be especially careful now, with Feardorcha camped a short march away, and Mathuin at his mercy," said Raemann.

"We're going to see Solomon again next Tuesday," said Fiona. "We promised."

"I don't know if that is such a good idea right now, Fiona. We can't really trust Varley. We all have to be really careful until we are sure about him," said Honora.

"I can trust Solomon though, and Flit and I are always careful," said Fiona.

"A friendship with Solomon could be a very good thing," said Raemann. "I think Flit and Fiona have proven they are worthy of our trust in their judgment."

That night I finished the necklace I had begun making for Cailean the day that Mathuin was taken from us. I gave it to her, an offering of something hopeful; a promise I could make to her about a future that we both wished for. I looked at Wilo's face across the room and the expression there was so sad, but not hopeless. She still held out hope for that dream too.

CHAPTER 22

THE MODEL BOY

When next Flit and Fiona met with Solomon, they found him busily engaged in building a model of his foster father's castle. He had paid special attention to the bridge that spanned the moat he had dug, a bridge that he could raise and lower, and with which he was hoping to impress his patron. He looked up at them with a dirt smudged face and tangled windblown hair, his cheeks ruddy with his efforts. Fiona thought him the most delightful boy she had ever seen. He seemed not to notice, but greeted them happily, and set about explaining what he had done so far, how everything worked, and what he had plans to finish yet.

When they approached him, he had been laying out the paths of the garden, and solicited their help in gathering plants of a size miniature enough to reproduce a smaller scale version of the great castle's walled formal garden. Fiona joined in wholeheartedly, leaving Flit to wander off in search of his brothers for some sport.

When the garden was finished to Solomon's satisfaction, they sat back for a bit to admire the creation, and decide what needed to be done next. The rooms had been roughed in approximately as they were positioned in the great castle. In his explanation of each room and each addition made to the castle, Solomon rehearsed for Fiona the history lesson he wished to recite for Lord Varley, including the significant contributions of each successive resident of the castle up to Lord Varley himself. Solomon showed Fiona where his room was located, in the east wing of the castle, where there were many grand but usually empty guest rooms. There, he told her, he could see the sun rise from his window. He had set his model up with a tiny bed made of sticks, a tiny table with an acorn cap for a washbasin and a bookcase with tiny books made of folded paper and stitched together with thread. Varley's private rooms were in the west wing, and Solomon had never been invited there, so he was not aware of how they were configured, but had simply recreated the same design in the west wing as in the east. There were two towers which Solomon had explored, and a great room or hall where visitors were entertained. There was a library as well, which Solomon had earned the privilege of using, when it became evident that he was inclined to treat the room and its contents with the respect they deserved. He had only to ask for a book on any given subject, and it was given to him to use and return.

Solomon had his run of the servant's quarters and the kitchen, and knew these rooms well. He had recreated them in detail, right down to the dishes and cooking utensils and tiny loaves of bread fashioned from clay. The servants had quickly drawn the engaging boy to their hearts and provided him with the warmth and affection he craved. It was evident to Fiona that the boy was thriving in his new surroundings, but his efforts to please his father seemed to have doubled with the negligence with which they were received. Fiona realized that the emptiest rooms were the rooms where he might be expected to have some contact with Lord Varley. Words could not have expressed more succinctly how the orphan fared at the castle. Still, Fiona was impressed with how well he seemed to be doing.

When Meagan, Solomon's governess, arrived to check on his work and accompany him back to the castle, Fiona greeted her warmly as an acquaintance she had run into occasionally in the village during happier times. Satisfied that his efforts would be found pleasing by his father, Solomon parted company with Fiona and headed back to the castle with Meagan, chatting happily about what Cook might have prepared for supper. Cook had developed quite a fondness for the boy and had an uncanny knack for knowing what would please him. His enjoyment of the treats she prepared was ample reward to the cook, who was as unused to a show of gratitude, as the boy was to being spoiled.

By the time Fiona found the brother foxes, the sun was riding low above the horizon, casting the long shadows of clouds across the hills. With the dying light reflecting like flames in the windows of the massive dark silhouette of the castle, Flit and Fiona headed back to the cave with thoughts of supper on their minds as well.

All was not deserted on the strand where the model of the castle awaited its inspection. Curious pixies, who usually danced upon that strand at night to the music of the crickets and grasshoppers, circled the model clucking and shaking their heads. Before long they were working with the industry of ants, transforming Solomon's working model into a fantastic creation, the like of which could only have originated in Faerie. Pleased that they had done the boy a great service, and exhausted with the work and the dancing, they assumed the shape of hedgehogs and waddled back into the flora and fauna as the sun's first rays illuminated their handiwork.

Later that morning Solomon approached with his father, riding his pony beside his father's large steed. The boy's heart was swelling with pride, as he had never before had the opportunity of riding with his father and he was certain that what he had prepared would please his father exceedingly.

The model could be seen at quite a distance now, its towers soaring high above the grasses of the meadow. Solomon's eyes were wide with astonishment, his mouth open in wonder. Varley's reaction was unequivocal.

"What enchantment is this?" he roared. Spurring his steed forward, he caused the enchanted castle to be trampled into the ground. Not a twig nor a plant remained of the boy's efforts nor those of the pixies. Handing the reins of the pony's bridle to one of his retainers, he commanded in a voice cold enough to freeze the very air they breathed; "Take the boy home. He is not to leave the castle. His lessons will be conducted there from now on."

Solomon stayed in his room all night and refused to come down to the kitchen, though the servants begged him. Cook made him up a tray with some of his favorites, but they went untouched. Meagan was relieved of her duties and sent packing the very next day. A new teacher replaced her, a stuffy gentleman whose lessons promised to be deadly dull and his methods unrelentingly strict. When the next Tuesday came and went, Solomon despaired. His lessons were being held indoors, and there was no chance of seeing his new friends again. Meagan was gone, his father angry and withdrawn; displeased beyond the boy's comprehension of how to make it up to him. Solomon resolved to do what many youngsters before him have done. He decided to run away. He waited until all was quiet and dark in the huge castle, took with him only a warm jacket, the pockets stuffed with some of Cook's delicacies wrapped in handkerchiefs. He felt a lump form in his throat at the thought of leaving Cook. At the last moment he decided to take with him a small miniature portrait of Siobhan, which Varley had given him, as well. Then he slipped through the narrow window of his room, and down the thick vines of ivy that covered the outer walls of the castle. While all within the castle slept, including the guard before his door, Solomon disappeared into the darkness on his way to find his friends and join the resistance.

CHAPTER 23

THE PHOOKAS

The dark shapes, two of them, hunched nearly invisible in the dark mass of the ancient tree, huge wings pulled in against the matted fur of their torsos. The glowing red eyes scanned the horizon, until movement in the waving grasses of the meadow riveted their attention; a small figure was approaching their perch from the direction of Castle Varley.

A small human shape appeared and stopped to rest under the immense tree, surveying the darkness of the landscape that closed in around him. When Solomon had left the castle, he had been quite sure of the direction he had seen Flit and Fiona head off toward, when they had parted company. He had been confident that he would be able to find them. Now it was dark and he was confused. He was no longer sure if he was headed toward his friends or away from them. He was tired, and scared, and he was hungry. Sitting down with his back to the great tree trunk, he retrieved one of the handkerchief-wrapped bundles of Cook's goodies from his pocket, and began to eat, spreading the handkerchief out on the ground before him as a tablecloth. Without warning, the female Phooka swooped down, and clutching the terrified boy by his jacket with her huge claws, swept away with him. Her mate picked up the remainder of the boy's meal and made quick work of it, leaving behind the fine linen handkerchief with the crest of the House of Varley embroidered upon it. They flew off together and disappeared into the inky blackness of the night sky.

Finn and Flann, out on a nightly hunting expedition, had spotted the boy, who appeared to be a friend of Flit and Fiona. They had been following a safe distance behind in the tall grass as the boy made his way toward the sentinel tree. They smelled the Phooka's sulphur smell before they saw their silhouettes move and separate themselves from the outline of the tree. But they were already too late. The boy was gone. Finn snatched up the handkerchief and they both darted away toward the cave of the fugitives.

Fiona was heartbroken.

"We've got to do something," she said, to the group gathered around Finn and the handkerchief he had brought back to the cave. He told her what had transpired and she had relayed it to the fugitives.

"If a Phooka kidnaps a human child there isn't much we can do about it, I'm sorry to say," said Raemann. "We would have no way of finding them. They are beyond our ken."

"Solomon isn't just a human child, he is Faerie as well. We have to hope that Solomon will be able to defend himself," said Wilo.

"But he's just a boy, and he has had no training," said Fiona, with a catch in her throat.

An orphan since before her memory of a mother or father, Fiona had never thought of herself as "just a child," even while she was not much older than Solomon herself. She was mother to all the lost and orphaned creatures she found.

"He's been trying so hard to please his human father, I don't think he's given a thought to his Faerie gifts," said Fiona.

"Yes, and that is probably just as well with a father like Lord Varley who is practically rabid about all things Faerie," I offered.

"Shouldn't we let Varley know what's become of the boy?" someone asked.

"Yes of course," said Honora, "the safest way to do that is through the fortune teller. He seems to trust her."

"Cailean, are you ready to ride?" asked Raemann.

"Anything is better than this waiting," said Cailean. "I am ready now."

As Solomon related the story to us later, he didn't seem unduly frightened, but viewed the countryside he was transported over, with dispassionate interest. He hadn't had time to be afraid before the Phooka swept down to grab him. He hadn't been devoured immediately, so he understood that the huge creatures had some other purpose for him. What that purpose was would be revealed to him soon enough. Meanwhile he made note of every geological feature that might afford him some sense of direction if he should be lucky enough to escape.

An untidy nest of driftwood, laced together and lined with seaweed, was the Phooka's destination. The nest was set into the craggy bluff of a sea wall, with crashing waves below. It contained three Phooka hatchlings, noisily demanding to be fed. It occurred to Solomon that this was meant to be his fate. The hatchlings were gawkier and uglier versions of their parents, with tufts of fur/feathers only half grown in, to cover their scrawny bodies and ungainly wings. Their large beaks were opened to let out a raucous chorus that demanded to be ceased with a meal. Their glowing red eyes, newly opened, focused weakly on the new inhabitant of the nest. Solomon inched to the farthest edge of the nest that hung out over the ragged rocks and the sea below. One of the hatchlings hiccuped, and in doing so changed into the form of a small pony, which tried unsteadily to stand on its wobbly legs. Solomon laughed at the comical sight, causing the other two hatchlings, startled, to change form also.

Phookas are accomplished shape shifters, usually taking on the shape of a small horse or pony, luring unsuspecting humans into wild rides, from which they frequently never returned. Another favorite guise is of a creature with the head of a goat and the body of a human. These newly hatched Phookas hadn't yet learned to shape-shift at will.

One of the hatchlings, with the body of a human baby, and the head of a young goat with nubs of horns protruding from its forehead, crawled toward Solomon and gave him a butt with its head that sent the boy flying from the nest. Seeing that their offering had been rejected, and the hatchlings had resumed their former shape and disturbing squawking, the adult Phookas flew off in search of a more acceptable means of quelling the clamor.

Solomon clung to the side of the nest until the adult Phookas were out of sight. Then he climbed around the nest to the ledge supporting it and pulled himself laboriously up the rocky face of the cliff to the top, where he stood for a moment to get his bearings. He followed a deer trail where it led off into the woods until it disappeared into a thicket. There he curled up to sleep for the night. Unbeknownst to Solomon, numerous pairs of eyes watched over him, most of them friendly.

Alarmed by Cailean's report of what had happened to Solomon, the old gypsy took out her crystal ball. In it she could see the boy curled up asleep in the thicket. From the mists swirling around him in the crystal orb, she could catch glimpses of the animals and faeries that watched over him, and one pair of eyes that alarmed her. Then the image swirled and faded. She and Cailean set out immediately for Castle Varley.

Varley was beside himself. When the boy was discovered missing, he had set out with his men and tracked him to the giant oak, where the trail disappeared. The trackers had pointed out Phooka droppings and he had feared the worst. Another member of his house had been attacked by an unnatural creature, and he had not been able to prevent it. Back at his castle, and in the blackest of moods, he paced. His helplessness at being able to protect his young charge fueled his rage. When the old gypsy and her young companion appeared at his doorstep unbidden, he demanded to know what had become of the boy. The old woman showed him the image in the crystal ball.

He seemed relieved to know that the boy was apparently still alive.

"Where is this thicket in which he sleeps?" Varley asked her.

"The faeries know," she responded.

He seemed to realize that he would be crossing a barrier with his next question and struggled with himself internally before he asked it.

"How do I make contact with the faeries?"

"You must travel with someone they trust," she replied.

"Do you know of someone who would be willing to accompany me?" he asked.

"I know someone, Lord Varley. If you would give me two horses, I could be back with him by first light, and ready to ride with you," this spoken by Cailean.

He looked at her intently.

"Who is this person?" he asked of her.

"It is Brennan, son of Oona, whose mother you killed," she replied.

Varley looked crestfallen and then desperate.

"Why would Oona's son be willing to help me,?" he asked.

"Because he is Oona's son," was her reply. This he seemed to understand.

Calling to his guards, he shouted; "Ready two horses for this young woman."

Knowing she wouldn't wish to inform him of Brennan's hiding place, Varley offered; "I presume you prefer to ride alone, rather than under guard?"

"That is the only way I would ride," she replied.

"Then go, and may Oona and my own dear Siobhan speed your way," was his response.

CHAPTER 24

JENNY GREENTEETH

When Solomon woke, it was to the sound of birdsong, and the first light of morning. He opened his eyes, and sitting on a stump directly in front of him, a squirrel nibbled on an apple. The boy and the squirrel continued to stare at each other, the boy not moving anything but his eyes, the squirrel calmly munching on the apple. Solomon was indeed very hungry and would have liked to have known where the squirrel had found the apple. As soon as the thought entered his head, the squirrel winked at him and headed off, stopping every few feet to look back at the boy. It seemed to Solomon that the squirrel wanted him to follow. Solomon jumped up in pursuit of the squirrel, thinking the little animal might lead him to food. Sure enough, the squirrel led him to the most beautiful little apple tree with fruits of green, red, and yellow, and leaves of gold. Solomon was too hungry to be amazed at the sight of such a wonderful tree, only reached up to pluck several fruits to stuff in his pockets. He had taken a bite of the reddest one he could find before he heard the squirrel speak thus; "Since you have stolen fruit from my tree, without permission, you will certainly be punished."

"I'm sorry to have offended you," said Solomon. "I thought you were leading me to the apples. I would have asked your permission if I had thought you would have understood me."

"Insolent boy," said the squirrel, who wasn't really a squirrel after all, but a gremlin in disguise. He took his usual form now, that of a short twisted creature with a wide mouth and tiny eyes. "Your excuses won't help you now. You must pay for the fruit you have taken or suffer the consequences."

"How do I repay you?" The boy asked.

"I need a bridge built across that river," said the gremlin. "At the narrowest part, there," he said pointing to a narrowing created by some large rocks and the roots of some willow trees which grew along the banks. The river rushed more quickly over the rocks and through the narrow opening. The water pooled blackly under the willow roots, and there, unbeknownst to Solomon, but very familiar to the gremlin, resided Jenny Greenteeth.

Solomon looked around him for anything he could use to build a bridge. Birch and willow saplings along the river banks could be laid down and secured with rocks to create a passable bridge.

"I could build a bridge if I had some tools," said Solomon. And then thinking quickly, he added; "that is, if I have your permission to cut down some of those saplings."

The gremlin seemed irritated that the boy was thinking so clearly.

"Here," he said, tossing the boy a knife he pulled from its sheath at his side. "You can use this, but mind you return it."

Realizing that it would take him all day to cut enough saplings for the bridge with only the knife, Solomon set out to begin the task so that he could be done with it and on his way.

At the very same time a meeting was taking place that had been long overdue.

When Cailean explained to me that Lord Varley had requested help finding Solomon, and that she had suggested me, I must admit that my first reaction was not one my mother would have been proud of. The thought of riding beside the man who had killed my mother and plunged all of us into such misery, and offering him help, ignited such a revulsion in me that I had to struggle to fight it down. Fiona pleaded her little friend's virtues with passion, stating that if I did not go, she would go in my stead to find Solomon. In the end I realized, that going was what my mother would have asked of me, and maybe the only way to end this cycle of fear and hatred. Still I was not prepared to meet his gaze for the first time.

Having been appraised of our approach, Varley and his retinue met us on the highroad. Approaching on horseback with his soldiers on either side and behind him, Lord Varley cut an imposing figure. As Cailean and I approached he lifted his gloved hand to halt those behind him and dismounted. His eyes searched out mine, met my gaze and held it. I don't know what he saw there, but I know it wasn't anger, for I felt none. In his eyes I saw only sorrow, and maybe a shadow of fear. Then he knelt on one knee before me and begged my forgiveness. If I had ever wanted to kill him, that would have been my chance, as he was helpless before me. Of course Cailean and I would have been dead before his body hit the ground, along with all of our hopes for a peace. But I didn't need to think these thoughts through. I pitied the man and forgave him, knowing that I would never again fear him.

Dusk was approaching, and Solomon, weary with the effort, was nearly finished with the bridge. The gremlin watched him greedily because with this task complete, he would be forgiven his debt to Jenny Greenteeth. The bridge was a spot which could be frequented by children on their way from school and town on one bank, and their homes on the other. They wouldn't have to walk so far to the high bridge. And Jenny liked children. She liked them very much indeed. Their ankles would be just within reach as they crossed the bridge with their thoughts on supper waiting at home, on kittens and puppies and hopscotch. There was one waiting for her right now. An earnest, rosy-looking boy, working so hard all day to build her bridge. He would be the first. She could hardly wait!

We had headed out toward the coast. When we were no longer within sight of the castle, and approaching an ancient graveyard, one that faeries frequent, I sang one of the songs I had learned from Wilo in the Faerie tongue. Out from behind a gravestone peered a faerie who flew to inches before my face.

"I know you, it's Oona's son you are. Why do you travel with the enemy? Are you his captive?"

"We have made a truce," I replied. "I am to help him find his foster son Solomon, a child of the mort-sidhe. Have you seen him? It is believed that Phookas took him."

"I haven't seen him, but I know someone who has," the little person replied. Then he flew off.

Varley looked at me as if to ask direction.

"We will proceed," I offered in response. "The faeries know where to find us."

Before long the faerie returned with another, who led us off toward the deep wood. Varley and his men looked nervous. I reassured them as best I could, wondering all the while if we weren't to be tested first before we were trusted.

At the deepest most sacrosanct part of the forest, a place of ancient trees casting deep shadows upon mossy boulders, an expectant stillness came over our surroundings. The striated beams of daylight were filtered and transformed like light through a cathedral window. The soldiers, and even the horses, were uneasy and on guard. Gradually, a dun colored ring of mushrooms, around us on the forest floor, began to glow and slowly circulate as it rose to encircle us. Within the glow we began to distinguish the faces and forms of hundreds, maybe thousands, of faerie folk, laughing and dancing, and making faces at us and the astonished soldiers. We were inside a faerie ring, but instead of forcing us to dance with them, the faeries were projecting each of our greatest fears, in hologram, into the circle. There appeared banshees, and goblins, a wasted old man with a long beard in a debtor's prison, a woman with a frying pan and a very disagreeable expression, several images of Feardorcha, someone trapped inside a burning building, and swirling in front of Lord Varley—black waters pulling someone down. Neither Cailean nor I showed the slightest fear of Varley. Cailean's fear was for Mathuin, held captive by Feardorcha, and mine, of facing Feardorcha again; a miniscule fake wizard standing up against a mountainous Feardorcha, with the hopes of hundreds depending on me.

By this device the faeries were able to discern our motives. They could tell we were not Varley's captives. The faerie ring dissolved and disappeared, leaving behind the two faeries who had been our guides thus far. The shadows were growing deeper, and Varley, impatient to find Solomon, was growing restless. He knew his men would not want to be in the forest past nightfall. The faeries assured Cailean and me that we hadn't much farther to go.

Solomon had just finished securing the saplings in place for his bridge. He had paused to survey his handiwork, wishing that his father could see what he had done. Tired, hungry, and another day behind on his quest, he sat down on the bridge, removed his shoes and socks, and dangled his feet in the pool of water by the willow roots. That was just too much temptation for Jenny Greenteeth. She grasped the unsuspecting boy by the ankles and yanked him hard.

As we approached the river, we heard a startled scream and saw Soloman's curly head disappear below the dark water. Without hesitation, Varley spurred his horse forward, and not stopping to remove his heavy coat of chain mail, leaped from his horse and into the pool. There was a violent thrashing and foaming of the water, and Solomon bobbed to the surface. Cailean and I each grabbed an arm and hauled him from the water, coughing and gasping for air.

The pool continued to boil for several minutes and then became deathly still. We all stood stunned on the riverbank for a long while, then searched both sides up and down until long after we knew there was no hope left. Solomon cried for the loss of his father, and Cailean and I cried for Solomon. The soldiers were impatient to make the journey back before dark, so we dismantled the bridge and left a sign warning children not to linger there for fear of Jenny Greenteeth. We attached the sign to a post and planted it into a patch of clover, where we spotted numerous four leafed clovers. That way the goblin that had misled Solomon would not be tempted to remove it. Solomon left the Goblin's knife stuck into the signpost. Then we left that unholy place.

CHAPTER 25

THE NEW
LORD VARLEY

We rode with the soldiers and Solomon, back to Castle Varley, and parted company. In a highly unanticipated turn of events, an eight-year-old boy of mixed human and faerie blood, was now Lord of Varley Castle. All that the new Lord Varley wanted when we arrived back at the castle was to see Cook. He ran to the kitchen and threw himself into her arms and sobbed out his sorrow over his father's sacrifice. She fed him some warm milk with honey and bread with jam, then rocked him in her arms until he grew drowsy. Before he fell asleep, he asked if he might see Fiona and Flit in the morning. We assured him that we would send them. Then Cook and the maid took him upstairs and tucked him into a warm bed.

When Cailean and I arrived back at the cave well after dark, the others were waiting for us. Several of the gypsies were there as well, including the old fortune teller. She had seen Oona and Siobhan in her crystal ball walking in the garden. With them was a third figure. It was Lord Varley. He had made it to the garden. She had known, before we had a chance to tell her, that Lord Varley was dead. Now we had to tell the rest of the story to the excited group around us. We talked well into the night about how this momentous change would affect our lives.

Because Varley's soldiers (now Solomon's soldiers) were familiar with Cailean and I, we accompanied Flit and Fiona to the castle in the morning, as the new lord had requested.

He greeted us solemnly, but was overjoyed to see Fiona and the fox. Fiona seemed to have the words to comfort him. We left them under an arbor and wandered together among the fragrant blossoms of Siobhan's garden, thinking of her, and how she loved the place; of her friendship with my mother in that other garden since her death, and of Varley's presence among them. It seemed a miracle too strange to fathom, and if I was jealous of Varley's presence with my mother, I was comforted too with the thought that someday I would be reunited with her and all of the others that Varley's vengeance had caused to be removed too soon from our lives. I didn't have Varley to hate anymore, but the injustice of his reward felt like a cinder burning in my heart. Left to smolder there, the only damage it would do, would be to my own spirit. Cailean sensed the struggle going on within me. She stopped walking and looked into my eyes.

"Brennan, when I first met you, I saw a boy with haunted, wounded eyes, who stood back and observed the world and the people in it with sadness and reservation. And yet there was kindness and caring there too. I have never heard you speak an unkind word to anyone. I think I fell in love with you when you first stumbled out of Wilo's cart full of cabbages. You had the look of someone that no amount of indignity could possibly make ridiculous, because it couldn't begin to compare to the depth of sadness that you had experienced. I don't think you have any idea how much your presence grounds all of us, how much you inspire us with your struggle to remain thoughtful, and caring, with all of the anger and madness swirling around us. You are our peace. Your presence is our safe harbor. We need you Brennan."

Tears welled up in her eyes, and I took her in my arms. Her tears fell on my chest, extinguishing the burning lump of blackness in my heart, and replacing it with a soft glow.

Fiona, Flit and Solomon found us there, our arms about each other, her head on my chest. Fiona looked at us curiously with a hint of mischief in her eyes. "Are we interrupting anything?" she asked.

We drew ourselves up and took a step away from each other.

"No Fiona, we are at your disposal," I said with a bow and a sigh.

"Good, because Solomon wants to help us get Mathuin back." she stated proudly.

"We all appreciate your intentions Solomon, but I don't know if you realize how dangerous that will be. Feardorcha is a very powerful wizard," I said.

"I've been thinking about it all morning," said Solomon. "Now there are soldiers to help."

"Do you think the soldiers can be trusted?" asked Cailean.

"The soldiers have no love for Feardorcha either, but fear is a strong motivator. The key rests with their captain. If we can trust him the others will follow."

"Not to worry Brennan. Cook says her son was just like me when he was little," said Solomon.

"What do you mean Solomon?" we both asked in unison.

"Cook says her son, Captain Saunders, was just like me when he was little."

"Well then, we have it beat," said Fiona laughing, "because everyone knows there's only one person in the world that loves Cook more than Solomon, and has more of a place in her heart, and that's her son, Captain James Saunders!"

To draw us out, Feardorcha had taken to parading Mathuin around about the perimeter of the camp in chains, under heavy guard, and announcing his challenge for the Wizard of Oona's Yew to come forward and do battle with Feardorcha himself. Messengers, both animal and human, were sent to our friends and allies in the forests and faerie glens, the towns, and in hiding; that Varley was no more, and the time had come to stand. The evening of the third night after his death would give us time to amass at the edge of the forest, from which we could see the tents and campfires of Feardorcha's encampment. Rowena's archers were there in force, demanding a place at the front of the lines. Solomon's soldiers, led by Captain Saunders, were waiting out of sight on the other side of Feardorcha's encampment. We hoped that the element of surprise that their addition to our numbers provided, might be what we needed to overcome our disadvantage in strength and numbers. We had another surprise for him as well.

At dusk, Feardorcha was issuing his challenge to the Wizard of Oona's Yew, heaping insults upon him for his lack of response. His soldiers were abusing Mathuin in the most heartrending manner, hitting him and spitting upon him where he stood, subdued and in chains. Before Feardorcha had quite finished, a cloud of bats numbering in the thousands, swooped out of the forest and began to create chaos among the soldiers, flapping their huge rubbery wings near the soldiers faces, and distracting them from Feardorcha's performance.

Feardorcha himself was riveted by the appearance of the bats. He knew they were a prelude to what he had invited, and stood his ground, his senses heightened. He scanned the periphery of the forest and saw a movement from the corner of his eye that caused him to focus on the forest edge just off center of the encampment. It appeared to his unbelieving eyes that a part of the forest floor had risen and begun to move. As he watched, the leaves and grasses and hollowed logs continued to rise and move in a sinuous snake-like manner, until the form began to take the shape of a dragon. The huge slithering thing poured toward him and rose up emitting a horrible smell worse than the direst bog. In chains beside the dragon, her head bowed in submission, stood Wilo. From the depth of the furnace in the monster's belly he belched his reply to Feardorcha's challenge, emitting sparks with each breath;

"I, Regneva Serutan, the Wizard of Oona's Yew, accept the challenge of Feardorcha, and offer this rebel captain and Faerie collaborator, known as Wilo, as your prize, should I lose. If I should defeat the mighty

Feardorcha, I call to witness all of your followers and all you see before you; that the captive Mathuin will be mine."

Feardorcha encircled Mathuin with his wand, and mumbled something unintelligible. Mathuin's body strained backward, fighting the force that propelled him. Then, under Feardorcha's direction, he slowly began to rise, and turn horizontally, until he stayed suspended, out of our reach, above one of the huge campfires, turning slowly like a roast on a spit. The whole forest erupted with the outraged cries of faerie, man, and beast, as they witnessed Feardorcha's handiwork. He seemed to react with some surprise at the volume of response, then turned to face the dragon-wizard and addressed him;

"I have waited a long time to meet again, what the people call, 'The Wizard of Oona's Yew,'" he said, taking in the craggy head, with knotholes for eye sockets, and the limbs of gnarled logs. He slowly approached Wilo and stood before her. He reached out and lifted her chin up so that her eyes, which had been averted, were now blazing at him.

"I am pleased that you should have thought to bring me the lovely Wilo as compensation for my trouble. Was that your idea or hers? Wilo and I are well acquainted. We are, you might say, family, are we not, my dear?"

Wilo's eyes, which bore through him with contempt, underwent a transformation that left little doubt as to the battle going on within her for her heart over her will. Head down, her shoulders slumped, she said;

"If you release Mathuin, I will go with you without a fight."

Feardorcha threw back his head and laughed contemptuously.

"Your audacity has always amused me Wilo, but what fun would there be in that? Besides, it seems to me that all I need to do is defeat this so-called dragon made of sticks and grass and I will have everything I want free for the taking. The people will know who is their master once again, and I will even an old score with you. It would seem that Mathuin means something to you! How better to see you suffer!"

With that he outstretched his arm and pointed at the fire below Mathuin. The flames leaped up alarmingly high, so that they must have singed his hair and clothing. Mathuin grimaced but uttered not a sound.

Then to the dragon Feardorcha spoke; "Come out of hiding and approach me, wizard to wizard, and we shall see, once and for all, who deserves allegiance!"

"Release Mathuin and you shall have your contest," blasted the voice of the dragon, emitted with smoke and flames enough to produce an awed response among Feardorcha's followers.

"You may release him yourself, if you best me in this contest," Feardorcha replied with a wicked grin. "Don't worry, you have some time, I've set him to a slow roast," Then he sent out a blast of flames that set the gnarled log that formed the dragon's head ablaze.

CHAPTER 26

A NEW BEGINNING

Inside the body of the dragon all was confusion. The hollow logs, gnarled branches, and dried grasses, that formed the exoskeleton of our dragon, were ready tinder for the fire that quickly erupted and soon engulfed our creation head to tail. Eyes blinded with smoke, the creatures inside abandoned what would have become their funeral pyre, and scattered in all directions, with little more than singed fur and minor burns. But that was not the end. A strong wind fanned the flames into a conflagration, and sent it barreling across the dry grass toward the encampment of Feardorcha's minions.

Our first thought, without exception, once we were free of the flames, was for Mathuin. In the confusion that the fire caused, while his soldiers were in disarray, there was a brief moment where it seemed possible to save him. But Feardorcha was single-minded in his resolve. He couldn't contain his followers, but he did have control yet in one arena. He had Mathuin's fate in his hands and he wasn't letting go.

Feardorcha's soldiers fled the fire, dropping their weapons in their panic and fear of the flames. Those that escaped the fire, were cut off by Rowena's archers, or enveloped by Solomon's army. The fire burned for hours until a cold wind blew in a steady rain. It rained all night, and in the morning, when we arrived at the spot where Mathuin had been suspended above the bonfire, there was nothing but ashes, long past smoldering.

It was a victory of sorts, but I can honestly say that no one felt like rejoicing. Feardorcha and his followers were gone, but so was Mathuin, and we knew not where. Had his spirit departed us forever? Or did he languish somewhere yet, in a prison of Feardorcha's design, while that cruelest of wizards awaited yet another chance to display his power over us all.

We met, factions of all of the rebels; the cave-dwellers, the Faeries, the mortals, the mort-sidhe, the animals, the gypsies, and young Lord Varley, and his representatives. It was a celebration, if a solemn one. We all knew that it wasn't finished, but in a sense, it was a new beginning. We felt a growing sense of our own power, when united for a single purpose.

In my dreams I replayed the confrontation; accepting Feardorcha's challenge, the sight of Mathuin spinning slowly above the fire, Wilo's defiance and resignation, Feardorcha's malevolence and determination. He had said they were family. What did he mean? Then the fire; and I saw my mother Oona, gently fanning the flames, blowing them in the direction of Feardorcha's camp, laughing and dancing gracefully in the rain.

Everyone wanted to know the answer, but no one wanted to ask it. What had Feardorcha meant when he said that he and Wilo were family? I waited until we were alone to ask her.

"Feardorcha was married to my sister Rozanna, Fiona's mother. She loved him very much, and very unwisely, as it turned out. Feardorcha was once a trusted emissary of the Faerie king, sent to watch over the king's family in their exile. For a time he performed that duty very well, and was rewarded, by the king, with powers beyond those of most wizard and faerie alike. They were meant to be used in defense of his family. He was granted those powers, and a limited immortality, in return for his service. It seems that the challenge of living several human lives is too much of a temptation for some mortals. He wasn't satisfied with what he had, and began to desire more power. I tried to warn Rozanna about him, but she always defended him. I should have understood how difficult it would be for her to oppose him. When she finally did stand up to him, and attempt to turn him from his ways, he told her she was dead to him, and had her locked away, never speaking to her again. When my father and mother came to bring her home to us, he wouldn't release her, but fought my father to the death. Rozanna did die soon enough, of a broken heart, but not before their daughter was born. My mother was there to hear her parting words, and to escape with the infant. Rozanna's last request of me, was that I see to it that Feardorcha would never find Fiona. Feardorcha doesn't know about her, and he must never know. Feardorcha is much more powerful than I am, but I have made it my life's mission to hinder him in any way that I can. I have always been proud to say that I have earned the animosity he feels toward me, but now

I can see that he has only turned it against those that I love."

Feardorcha and his followers were gone. We lived for some time, as we had before, underground, and in fear of his return. We knew he would return. Gradually we gave up the old ways. We came up into the sunlight. We were aided in this by the young Lord Varley, Solomon. He set his soldiers to work helping us rebuild our homes. We planted crops and gardens and nurtured them and our own dreams of a better life. Raemann and Honora got their farm back, as did many others who had lost theirs. School resumed for the children.

Wilo found a place for herself there teaching the young ones. It was the only place where I could sometimes still see glimmers of the old Wilo's natural humor and commanding presence. The villagers, grateful for all she had done, provided her with a cottage—probably the first home she could remember calling her own. She lived alone and avoided the company of others. I would sometimes see her walking the dusty road from the schoolhouse to her lonely cottage in the woods, with a far-off look in her eyes, or on the bluff overlooking the village, as she restlessly paced, scanning the sky or the horizon. Despite the affection they held for her, she made people nervous. They had lived a long time in fear and didn't want to be reminded. They wanted to move on, and she wasn't going to forget.

CHAPTER 27

WILO

Wilo stayed with us until that next fall. Then, just before the school year was to begin, she disappeared. Her cottage stood empty, except for a few meager pieces of furniture; the door ajar, leaves swirling around the bare interior, through the breeze from an open window. She had told no one of her plans, and left us no information about where to reach her. Flit and Fiona moved in to keep the cottage for Wilo's return.

Wilo and I had exhausted every lead we had about Mathuin's fate. No one; not animal, faerie nor mortal, seemed to have a clue about what had become of him. Many mourned him as dead. I was not one of those, nor was Wilo, but we seemed to have come up against a brick wall in our efforts to locate the smallest trace of him. I knew how dreadfully she missed him, and how thoughts of his suffering tortured her. I was not really surprised to find her gone. She knew Feardorcha better than anyone else, and I think she felt that his not showing up was a sign to her that she must seek him out. It was very like Wilo to feel she had to do this on her own, without endangering anyone else. She must have uncovered a lead that she was now following up. Since she had chosen not to inform me, I had to be patient and wait. I was to find that waiting can sometimes be more difficult than taking action.

The villagers were preparing for their first Christmas since the liberation. Fresh snow covered the cottages in thick drifts up to the windowsills, and sparkled in the blue shadows cast by moonlight. The warm amber light spilling from the interiors through frosted windows, beckoned all who might yet be out and about, to hurry home and join the festivities. At Raemann and Honora's homestead, they waited with Cailean for me to return from my job at the booksellers. Raemann and Honora had insisted that I resume residence in the old room that I had shared with Mathuin. I had helped Raemann put up his crops in the fall, and when the opportunity presented itself for work at the booksellers, I had taken it. The additional income that I might contribute was part of my decision, but more importantly, it provided ready access to news and events in the village and beyond.

As I approached home, I could see Honora and Cailean in the window, bustling about as they prepared the table for dinner. Raemann was in his favorite chair close to the fireplace, smoking his pipe. It presented such a picture as anyone would be pleased to be approaching, yet I knew the individuals and how each was doing their best to present the illusion of normalcy and cheer in spite of the fact that their hearts were frosted over in grief. Their hands went about their chores because it helped to move them through another day without news of Mathuin.

Cailean greeted me at the door and took my coat. She hung it up. She turned slowly and her eyes searched out mine, as they had on so many previous days, looking for some hint of hope. Lately I had taken to preparing my expression to meet hers before I entered the door. This put a strain between us, her expecting, and me disappointing.

The women had outdone themselves with their preparations for the holiday dinner. The aroma wafting from the warmth of the hearth was very inviting. We sat down to dinner and all three pairs of eyes turned toward me, as I recounted my day.

"There have been no reports from our compatriots outside the country, and my father has had no word of any disturbance among the animals" I advised them.

Daily reports were sent, along with shipments of books and newspapers, by Mathuin's friends in far-flung places. My father had decided to stay in the village and minister to the people there, but he was in contact with the monastery and a wide network of animal friends.

"And I have received no word from the gypsies either," said Cailean.

"I suppose we ought to take comfort in the thought that all is well among so many," offered Honora.

"Yes," said Cailean, "I don't know why I am having such a difficult time looking at the positive side of things. To think I used to abuse you about it, Brennan. I don't know how you put up with me."

"The time I spent with you always afforded me the most hopeful moments in the darkest of times, Cailean.

Which is why it is so hard for me to have to disappoint you day after day," I told her.

Honora reached out and took each of our hands in hers. "We all know how hard you are working to find out news of Mathuin," she said.

"It's the not knowing that is the hardest part to bear," said Raemann. He seemed to have aged ten years in the last year, his hair and beard sprinkled with grey. His usually hearty manner had taken on an uncharacteristic gravity that was sometimes hard to penetrate.

An unexpected knock on the door startled us all from our seats. Honora reached the door first and opened it to find Wilo standing on the doorstep, her silvery blond hair, and her shoulders, covered in a velvet cape, dusted with snow crystals.

"Wilo!" she shouted, grabbing her, and pulling her inside into a warm hug, and then more hugs from the rest of us. "You're so cold! Warm up here by the fire first while we set another place for you at the table," said Honora, as she took Wilo's cape and hung it on a peg near the hearth.

Happy to have the attention drawn from me, I joined the others in my anticipation of whatever she might have discovered of Mathuin's fate.

Wilo had been revisiting places she knew to be haunts of Feardorcha's, from the days when he had been married to her sister Rozanna. Each stop stirred up painful memories of her sister, and their former happy life, and Feardorcha's transformation and betrayal. Their honeymoon cottage, where their first happy years had been spent, was now an uninhabited tangle of vines and thorns. The place by the seashore where their extended family had spent many happy summers, had been destroyed by a storm, with little trace left of its existence but some weathered timbers. The mountain fortress, which Feardorcha had reinforced in the later years, and had spent progressively more time in, had become Wilo's center of focus. It was here, where her sister had been least happy, that Feardorcha had finally chosen to lock her away. It was here that Wilo suspected he might have done the same with Mathuin. Feardorcha was a powerful wizard, and he could have chosen a spot undetectable by anyone, with the many enchantments at his disposal. Wilo felt that her knowledge of her sister's fate at the fortress was reason enough for Feardorcha to hold Mathuin there; he had baited the trap, and had only to wait for her to take the bait. She had more than just a hunch to go by; Feardorcha had left an unmistakable sign of Mathuin's presence, that she alone could read. From the window of the same tower room where her sister had been imprisoned, flew an unusual banner. It was a jersey that Wilo had made for Mathuin in his favorite colors, blue and yellow. The message was a cruel and taunting challenge.

Wilo was back now at her cottage and we were grateful that Fiona and Flit remained there with her for company. Still she would disappear without a word to anyone and be gone for several days at a time. The blue and yellow jersey, faded and tattered now, continued to agitate her, as it fluttered incessantly in her mind's eye. We were certain her trips away were to try and figure a way into that fortress.

CHAPTER 28

ROWENA

Rowena's significance among the townspeople had increased immeasurably after the defeat of Feardorcha's army. No one could help but acknowledge the part that Rowena's archers had contributed. Because of this, and perhaps because they felt guilty for having misjudged her, labeling her as the daughter of thieves, she received many offers of employment. Rowena considered each offer thankfully, but settled on the one which, while it didn't offer the highest wage, interested her the most. She was to apprentice with the woman that most of the townspeople looked to for help with medicines and ailments.

Miss Witherspoon, in her younger years, had apprenticed with her predecessor, who had passed the knowledge on to her. Now advanced in years, she was looking for a suitable pupil who might become a repository of that knowledge, and had the energy and desire to use it for the common good. She had chosen Rowena, and Rowena had accepted with gratitude. She was given a room in her benefactor's home as her own, the first such space she had ever had to call her own, and made to feel needed and welcome. While the home was far from grand, it was very comfortable, and sufficient to both their needs. Her education began without more delay. Rowena accompanied Miss Witherspoon on her rounds of home-bound villagers, and made forays with her into the countryside for medicinal herbs. Any rare ingredients they couldn't supply on their own could be found at the pharmacist's in town, as he had contacts with suppliers in distant ports. Anyone who hadn't known Rowena before, was soon to know her in her new capacity, as Miss Witherspoon's assistant. Evenings, when they weren't called out for an emergency visit, they could be found pouring over volumes in Miss Witherspoon's extensive library.

I saw Rowena most frequently when she came to town to pick up something from the pharmacist's shop, as the bookstore was right next door. She would usually stop in to say hello, while she was waiting for her script to be filled. Her good fortune had not caused her to forget her friends, and her first concern was always for any news of Mathuin.

Besides Mathuin's own family, and of course Wilo, there were few people I trusted more than Rowena. I told her of Wilo's suspicions when next I had the opportunity to see her. Her dark eyes glowed with intensity as I described the fortress, a sinister looking place which appeared to have formed itself from the native rock of the island from which it thrust itself upward, and crouching, surveyed the waters surrounding it like a living thing.

"And that gloomy place is where our Mathuin spends his days and nights apart from all who love him," said Rowena. And then more optimistically, "But Brennan, Mathuin is alive! This gives us real cause for hope that we may someday have him home with us again."

"Of course it is a trap set to entice Wilo," I allowed, "but just the same, it appears to confirm that what we all hoped to be true, really is, and Mathuin is alive."

A customer came in, causing the bell above the door to ring. I changed the subject of our discourse to another one, which I knew would interest Cailean and her parents.

"You are looking very well, Rowena, Miss Witherspoon must be an agreeable employer."

"She is wonderful, Brennan, so knowledgeable and patient. I know she could have found someone quicker than me, but no one so willing. And the people! They are so grateful. The little children are shy and in awe. I just have to do something to make them laugh and feel at ease. Would you believe, my juggling has been very useful! And I have my own room upstairs at Miss Witherspoon's, with a little lamp that has a clever bronze squirrel at the base eating acorns, and a cozy bed with a goose down pillow, and a comforter in my favorite shade of blue, and a bookcase for my books, and a cupboard for my clothes. My room overlooks our garden, where we grow some of our herbs, and most of the food we eat. If a family can't afford our fee, they send us home with a chicken, or some eggs, or maybe some salt pork, or baked goods. I have never been so busy or so happy."

Rowena paused then, her face pensive. "I wish my mother and father could be here to see me now. I would make sure they never had to want for anything."

Rowena stopped suddenly, as if feeling guilty for rambling on so. "Believe me, Brennan, when I say my present happiness doesn't cause me to forget what you and Cailean's family are going through. I want you and Wilo to know that whatever you decide to do, I'm in," she offered.

"I'll keep you posted, Rowena." I said this knowing that I would have to be hard pressed to involve Rowena in any schemes that would take her away from her new life, which she obviously relished, and was so deserving of.

CHAPTER 29

FIONA AND SOLOMON

Fiona had made a discovery in the forest behind Wilo's cottage. An ancient oak had been removed from there many years before, and it's moss covered stump, big enough around to set places for eight or more for a picnic on the forest floor, had become Fiona's favorite place to sit and ponder during the day, or stargaze at night. The ancient tree had become a subject of reverie for her, as she imagined its former glory, as host to animals of many kinds, the lofty views it must have had from its topmost branches, and what had become of its limbs and trunk. She wondered if the tree felt pain as it's limbs were removed one by one, and was finally truncated, and hoped that it had been put to some purpose worthy of such a venerable specimen, such as cross beams in a cathedral, or a beautifully carved alter, so that it's sacrifice might be immortalized somehow with comparable beauty and awe.

One day, absorbed in such thoughts and feeling especially connected to the tree, Fiona happened to think about her friend Solomon, whom she missed and thought of frequently, but rarely saw any more. Her thoughts took the form of a fervent wish to be in his presence, and without another thought, she found herself standing in the garden—Siobhan's garden. She stood there dazed for a moment in wonderment, looking about her in the garden, so full of beauty and life, but unsure what to do next; when around from a corner of the boxwood border came Solomon, and his mentor Captain Saunders. Both of them stopped in surprise, until Solomon, with a joyful yelp, recognized her, and ran to her side. They surveyed each other curiously for a moment, noting subtle differences that their time apart had wrought.

"You have more freckles," he stated, "I like them very much. And your cheeks are rosier."

"You don't tend to get as much sun when you spend most of your time in a cave," Fiona responded. "And you are a little taller. Your hair is shorter and neater. I kind of liked it all curly and rumpled, but it's wonderful to see you."

"I shall be rumpled whenever you like, and I will be, the next time I expect you. But you did surprise me. How did you get here Fiona? Who let you in? They should have announced you and brought you to me immediately."

"Captain, you remember Fiona," Solomon said, and as he introduced her, Captain Saunders swept off his hat and bowed.

"I do indeed sir, I know her to be a very good friend of yours, and if you like I will leave you two to your visit. I have those matters we were discussing to attend to."

"Thank you Captain."

"You were telling me how you got here Fiona."

"That's just it, Solomon," said Fiona, "I'm not at all sure how I got here, but I think I'm beginning to figure it out. I was sitting on the old oak stump behind Wilo's cottage, and I thought of you, and this place, this garden, and wished so much to see you, and here I am. I think the old oak is a portal and I somehow stumbled upon the secret to using it. I'm not sure how to use it in reverse. I don't know how to get home again. Could the garden itself be another portal?

"You will certainly have to try it when you wish to go home, but not yet! We need more time together. Where is Flit? How is the clever fellow?

"Oh, my goodness, Flit was lying in the grass by my feet. He must be looking all over for me. He is used to me miniaturizing. Maybe he thinks I'm playing hide and seek. He is happy about being outside whenever he likes. He goes to visit his brothers and Flossy and her family quite often. Sometimes I do too. They are just the same, except the little foxes, of course. They are growing so fast! You would love to see them. Do you ever have time for your sketching? You were so good at it. What are your days like? How is Cook?

"Wait, Fiona, one question at a time. I would love to see the little foxes and sketch them, but you are right I don't have much time to do many of the things I used to enjoy. There is so much to learn here, and many people depend on me to know about things which are important to them, so I feel I must learn how best to help them, not just one person at a time, but all of them at once. As soon as you think you know how best to solve one person's problem, you discover that same solution may work to someone else's disadvantage. It's very complicated. But I have people like Captain Saunders, who have been helping and advising me. There are the rebuilding projects that the soldiers are working on; many of them have families that need taking care of and the soldiers need something to do or they end up getting into fights with each other, or arguments with the villagers. Some of the villagers don't trust the soldiers and create more problems for all of us by insulting them whenever they get the chance. The rebuilding projects are helping with that problem, but everyone thinks their needs should take priority, so I have set up a council of villagers, led by Raemann and Honora, who sort through the requests and prioritize them. Then we need to have some kind of income in order to pay for all of our projects, the soldiers and farmers wages, and our taxes to the king. There are crops that we might try, that could sell better than the ones that had been grown before, and we are trying to come up with ways to encourage the peasants to earn land that they can take ownership of, and pride in rather than just living on the land and being unfairly taxed with no say, as they were before. I wake up early in the morning excited about seeing how much we can accomplish in the day. I fall asleep at night and find my dreams are continuing the work through the night."

"I can understand how involved you are in creating a better life for the people around you and in your charge. I am very impressed with how much you have done already, and with all you plan to do. It is no less than I would have expected of you. I don't know if you have heard this, but the townspeople refer to you as Solomon the Good!"

"Really, Fiona? Well I am certainly glad that you don't feel compelled to call me that. Cook already spoils me enough."

"And what of Cook, has she been well?"

"Cook is very well. She says she never expected to have her two 'boys' to make over the way she can now, meaning me and Captain Saunders of course. You have to stay to tea. She would be so disappointed if she heard you were here and didn't stop in to see her, and I know she would insist on tea. She will want to make something special to celebrate your being here. Lets go in and surprise her right now!"

Fiona was welcomed by Cook, with open arms and a warm hug. While the cook and the girl caught up on all of the happenings of the past few months, Fiona assisting with the preparations for tea, Solomon joined Captain Saunders and some of the local builders in the library to go over the reconstruction plans until tea was declared ready.

A table was set in the garden under a shady arbor, for the two friends who continued their visit, until Solomon was assured that Fiona had tried each of the delicacies and they had caught up on all of their acquaintances.

"So there is still no news of Mathuin," Solomon mused. "Have they tried the fortune teller? She was so helpful in the search for me when the Phookas took me."

"We tried that right away," said Fiona. "Feardorcha has obscured any messages she might have gotten in relation to Mathuin. The old gypsy's crystal ball just comes up cloudy. Wilo is certain that he is still alive, and being held at Feardorcha's Fortress."

"I have been studying sketches of the structures hereabouts. That particular fortress is built in a very secure location, with numerous defenses. It would be next to impossible to breach it," said Solomon.

"Yes, under ordinary means I suppose it is," said Fiona thoughtfully. "But what if there were a portal somewhere in the fortress. What if it could be entered as easily as I appeared here in Siobhan's garden? I mean your garden, of course."

"That's all right Fiona. I think it shall always be Siobhan's Garden. Your theory presents a very interesting dilemma for me defensively as well. Who else might know about these portals? We need to find out more about how they work. I'll see what I can find in my library. There are some very old, rare volumes that might contain answers, or at least steer us in the right direction."

"And I need to talk to Wilo. If anyone we know has knowledge about things of this nature it would be her. I think I had better try to get back home as soon as possible. I'm going to try to go back the way I came, but if that doesn't work I'll have to ask you for a lift home."

"Of course, Fiona, I'll be happy to arrange a ride for you, but I would really like to see how this portal thing works. You said you were sitting on the tree stump. What were you thinking?"

"Well, first I was feeling very attached to the tree, thinking good thoughts about it, and then I thought about you, and how much I missed you, and wished I could see you again. I think I even got a little teary."

"Really, Fiona?" said Solomon, looking pleased for an instant before he started to analyze what that could mean in terms of repeat patterns and reproducing the same result. "So it would seem that there are three major elements to consider; the proximity to a portal, some positive thoughts about the nature of the portal, and an emotional attachment to someone that you would like to be transported to. Does that about sum it up?"

"Yes, that is how it appears to me too, unless I am missing some subtle differences."

"Well, let's give it a go. Are you ready Fiona?"

"Let's see. I was standing right about here in the garden when I arrived. I shall think of Siobhan and how much she loved this place, how beautiful it is and worthy of admiration. Then I shall think of a loved one—Wilo—and a place to return to her—the oak stump behind her cottage."

Fiona stood with her eyes squeezed shut for a few moments. When she opened them she was still standing in the same spot in the garden.

Solomon said, "I think I should leave you for a little while so that you can practice getting into the frame of mind you need. I won't be far off. Good luck Fiona. We'll see each other again soon." With that he walked off to watch her, out of sight.

Fiona relaxed and tried again. This time when she opened her eyes, she was standing on the stump beside Wilo's cottage. Flit jumped up to greet her with an eager smile on his handsome face. They frolicked about in a happy dance around the stump, but stopped in shocked surprise as a familiar figure approached from around the front of the cottage.

"Fiona, you shouldn't have worried Flit and me like that," said Wilo. "Where were you? We have been looking all over for you."

"You're one to talk, Wilo! You disappear for days and weeks at a time without a thought to anyone else," replied Fiona, with an angry and indignant look on her face.

"Yes," said Wilo, "I suppose I had that coming. I promise to try and be more considerate."

"I will, if you will, Aunt Wilo. I don't know if you understand how much I worry about you when you disappear. You and Flit are my only family. If something happened to you I would be all alone in the world." Huge tears welled up in her blue eyes and spilled down her freckled cheeks.

Wilo was shocked. She was so used to seeing Fiona in her role as mother to all the little ones that she had forgotten how young Fiona was. She saw her for the first time as the vulnerable young girl she really was. Wilo sat down on the stump and pulled her niece next to her, and wrapped her up in her arms.

"I'm so sorry Fiona, please forgive me. I've been so wrapped up in my grief over Mathuin that I haven't been seeing clearly."

"I know, Wilo. But I need you too—and I have something to tell you. You asked where I was just now. I have returned from a visit with Solomon, and I didn't take any of the usual modes of transportation!"

"What are you telling me Fiona?"

"I am telling you that I discovered a portal into Siobhan's garden. It's this old oak stump!"

Wilo's eyes widened and then narrowed. "Of course, why didn't I think of that before?"

Now Fiona looked concerned. "What do you mean Wilo? You aren't thinking of using the portal to enter the fortress are you?"

"I am indeed, my clever little niece."

"It had occurred to me as well," said Fiona, "and I was intending to ask you just what you know about these portals and how they work. I don't want you to go dashing off without thinking it through thoroughly. The oak stump is a portal, and I think Siobhan's garden is one. They are both very powerful natural places. That is how I was able to go from one to the other and return. But if you are able to use the oak to get to Mathuin, and there is no portal in the fortress, you may both be held there with no way to return. Feardorcha may even have that very thought in mind, with his knowledge of Faerie. He may be waiting for you to let your frustration lead you to do something impulsive. You have to promise me you won't let that happen, Wilo."

Wilo looked at her niece fondly and replied; "I don't intend to do anything foolish Fiona. I want Mathuin back, and I want to be with him. I have heard of the portals, of course, I have even used a few of the more commonly known ones to get around. Oona's Yew and Siobhan's Garden are fairly recent portals. Some of them are very old. You are right that powerful sources of nature such as the ancient tree, or a waterfall, are typically used as portals, The site of momentous human events such as a battlefield can be as well. Sometimes they have certain specifics attached to them in order to make them less likely to be stumbled upon as you seem to have done. Feardorcha's fortress is built from rock, into a cliff face, above the pounding surf of the ocean. It may contain a portal. I can promise you I will be researching this very thoroughly."

"Very good. And Solomon is going to help. He has a very extensive library which may hold some of the answers we are seeking."

"All right Fiona, but we must keep this plan exceedingly private. Feardorcha is not without his eyes and ears in the community. We don't need to give them any leads to go on."

"Right, I agree Wilo, just you and me and Solomon, and Brennan and Cailean."

"Agreed."

"If you go I am going to go with you, Wilo."

"You definitely are not, Fiona."

"But it was my idea!"

"And I am grateful for it. But you are my responsibility, and you will be going nowhere near that place."

"When are we going to tell Brennan and Cailean?"

"There's no time like the present."

CHAPTER 30

PORTALS

When first asked to head the Council of Citizens, Raemann and Honora were reluctant to accept. Cailean recognized the inertia of sadness that was holding them back, and feared for them because of it. She worked on each of them separately, and their concern for the other, to get them involved. Once active in the pursuit of solutions for others, their own worries about Mathuin, while still of utmost concern to them, were no longer holding them back from living. Because the community was concerned about Mathuin as well, they received support from their friends and neighbors on a daily basis that helped make the task of fearing, but not knowing, easier to bear.

One of Honora's favorite projects was finding homes for the many orphans and matching them with families that best suited each other's needs. Those families that had lost a major breadwinner, and were in danger of losing their homes as well, were of major concern to Raemann. He was constantly in contact with the banks, money-lenders, and business owners, to help work out payment plans. Meanwhile, widows, and sons and daughters, were being trained at new occupations, so that they could become self-sustaining once again. Another project they started was to organize a central location where any surpluses of grain, vegetables, dairy products, clothing, and household items, could be distributed to anyone in need. Rowena and Miss Witherspoon were involved in this exchange as well, providing advice and assistance where needed. The little community was starting to hum again.

At home the atmosphere was considerably brighter, and conversations revolved around the work being done, and progress being made. I felt the burden of providing a solution to their problems lift somewhat from my shoulders, and I began to look forward to being together in the evenings. Cailean was so relieved by the change in her parents, that she began to look her rosy self again. Sometimes in the evenings we would take the horses out for a ride together. We had a favorite spot to watch the sun set, and the stars come out one by one. In those times we dared to speak of our future together, so I knew that I still held her heart just as she held mine.

Wilo was a concern to both of us. She would not, or could not, put down her burden of sorrow. When next Wilo and Fiona came to visit, they were bursting with excitement about the discovery of the portal. Cailean and I were swept up in their enthusiasm. We didn't include Raemann and Honora in our discussions. We didn't want to get their hopes up before we were certain how to proceed.

Wilo was certain that Mathuin was being held in the room that had been her sister Rozanna's, in the tower; the place which had once been her sanctuary, and in the later days became her prison. There was not much danger if we were wrong about the location, the transport would simply not occur. Once inside, the danger increased considerably. We had many questions about how the portals worked.

We decided that our next meeting should include Solomon and any information he might have gathered from his library. We intended to attempt a group transport to Siobhan's Garden by way of the oak stump portal. The first opportunity to do so would be the week's end. We agreed to meet at Wilo's cottage on Saturday morning.

Saturday came, a fine day, and we were excited about the prospects. We had all foregone breakfast, not knowing if that would make a difference. We stood on the stump, holding hands, while Fiona talked us through her thoughts of reverence for the great tree that had once been, and we all envisioned Siobhan's Garden.

In a flash we were there, holding hands, waist deep in flowers and the scent of flowers, the sound of the busy worker bees humming in our ears, butterflies kissing the faces of blossoms, and skipping happily from one to the next.

Solomon had been researching the subject of portals. His primary discovery was a slim volume written in a spidery hand. It contained illustrations of several natural portals. Three of these, were easily recognizable locations, familiar to all of us; a cave with an entrance approachable at low tide, an ancient graveyard, and a grove of venerable trees. They became our playground—our practice field. With the information in the book, and various scenarios to explore, we began to develop a plan with a variety of options.

If Wilo managed to transport herself to the fortress portal, how could she best protect herself once there? If Feardorcha had set a trap for her, which he undoubtedly had, how best to elude him, and still escape with Mathuin? We now knew that it is possible to transport more than one person at a time, but what if Mathuin or someone else in the transport party were disabled? What if Feardorcha chose to follow us by using the portals himself? Was there a way to prevent him?

Using the book as a guide, and by trial and error, we discovered we could transport animals, namely Flit. But he didn't seem to have the ability, whether by lack of concentration or lack of visualization, to aid in the transport. It didn't work with just one or two to assist a disabled traveler, there had to be at least three. That was a major discovery. Now we knew that there would need to be at least three of us on our mission. After much trial and error and heated arguments on each side, it was agreed that Wilo, Cailean, and I would attempt the entry to the castle, and Fiona and Solomon would stay behind as support for our re-entry. Fiona wasn't happy about that, but Solomon's responsibilities, and also his resources in manpower, made it clear that he would be more valuable on this side. Wilo was insistent. She wouldn't have any part of Fiona being anywhere near Feardorcha. Solomon managed to convince her that her skills and knowledge of transporting were going to be crucial if there was a problem on the return. We practiced our skills at transporting under various conditions of weather, times of day and night, even phases of the moon. We visited all of the sights we were aware of, coming and going, until they became familiar. When we felt fairly comfortable with the sites we had access to, we set out to find the other sights illustrated in the book.

Wilo was getting restless to attempt the rescue. We had to keep convincing her that we hadn't discovered enough of the possibilities about the portals, that it was wiser to be patient, and better prepared.

"We will never be able to prepare enough for this," said Wilo. There will always be something we haven't thought of, and meanwhile, Mathuin suffers daily for our hesitation."

She had a point there, I had to admit, but I did feel we needed to have a plan ourselves that could be altered to fit the various courses that our actions might take once we were confronted by Feardorcha. Once we were inside the fortress we would no longer have the element of surprise working for us, and Feardorcha would have the advantage. We needed to have some more tricks up our sleeves, to buy us more time, once inside. I thought of Rowena and her burgeoning knowledge of medicinals.

CHAPTER 31

COLORED POWDERS

I hadn't seen Rowena for several weeks. I caught up with her in the garden at Miss Witherspoon's. I walked around to the back of the house, where I knew they had extensive gardens filled with herbs, edibles and medicinals. I found her crouching over a plant with a fine paintbrush, distributing pollen from one plant to another. She stood up, with a wide smile on her tanned and rosy cheeks, and gave me a huge hug. She smelled of earth and air and warm sun-kissed skin, and looked like mother nature herself. We walked, arm in arm, as she showed me around the gardens, and she explained what each plot was for, and how each plant was used. Rowena had pretty much taken over the gardening from Miss Witherspoon, who suffered now with arthritic joints. That left Miss Witherspoon more time for her cataloging and illustrations. She was preparing a book on medicinal herbs and native plants and their uses. I could see that Miss Witherspoon had chosen her apprentice wisely, and that their partnership was working out well.

I couldn't help but comment; "I can't tell you how pleased I am to see you looking so well, Rowena. You have truly found your place in the world."

"Yes, Brennan, I have never been so happy. It is a wonderful thing to be useful and respected, and doing what you love. But now I just know you have something to tell me about Mathuin," she coaxed, her large dark eyes bright with interest.

When I had filled her in on our plans to enter the fortress and rescue Mathuin, I asked her opinion on anything we could do to delay, obscure, defer, restrain, or immobilize, Feardorcha.

Rowena grew very serious. "I can think of a few substances that would have the effect you might wish, but most of them don't take effect immediately. I need to think about this more. I need to take Ms. Witherspoon aside and get the benefit of her experience. Give me a day or two and I will get back to you."

"I'm sorry to involve you in this Rowena," I offered.

"Please, Brennan, I'm honored to help in any way I can. I'm glad you included me.

If you need more than medicinal information I will be glad to help in any way I can."

"Thanks, Rowena," I responded, "There never was a better or more loyal friend than you."

Several days later, Rowena contacted me at the bookstore with the results of her inquiries. She handed me three pouches filled with powdered substances which had been ground from plant sources and dyed three different colors to distinguish one from the other.

"Each of the powders has a unique property, which you may find useful in eluding Feardorcha. Of course, we must assume that Feardorcha will be acquainted with these plants and their properties, and may be able to neutralize or circumvent them. To a large extent, their effectiveness will depend on the element of surprise. They will buy you some time. With a wizard as powerful as Feardorcha, that is about all you can expect. "I wish I had more to offer you. Miss Witherspoon and I have concentrated all our efforts on medicinals that will help people, and on undoing the effects of plants that shouldn't have been ingested. We don't do "Black Magic," in fact, what we do isn't magic at all. In her many years as a healer Miss Witherspoon has occasionally been called upon to relieve the effects of these powders I am about to explain to you."

She looked at me intently and I knew she was impressing upon me the importance of the oath she had taken, "to do no harm" and all that she was entrusting me with.

Then she began. "The blue powder, if ingested or absorbed into the skin, will cause a paralysis to occur and the affected person will appear to all outward signs to have died. There will be no apparent heartbeat or breathing, but the effect will wear off in approximately six hours. Sooner, if an antidote is applied. The red powder causes hallucinations which appear to be real in the most frightening way possible. They work differently with the mind of each person affected, to produce their own brand of nightmares. You can see how this might forestall an enemy for a time, if you need a diversion, but remember—it is temporary. The third powder, the green one, will require the recipient to speak only the truth. You may find this useful with guards or servants once you are inside the fortress. Usually the powders are mixed into food or drink. It is not very likely that you will be sitting down to dine with Mathuin's captor, nor will you be likely to have access to his food or drink. He is, after all, an individual that many people hate, including his servants, so it is not hard to imagine that he will have some poor expendable child of a servant as taster, to ensure his own safety. This being the likelihood, remember that the powders may be thrown into the eyes of the subject or absorbed through the skin, especially if diluted in a small amount of water."

"I can't thank you enough, Rowena, for all you have done." I told her.

"Without Miss Witherspoon, and her knowledge, I wouldn't have been much help at all," said Rowena.

"I am indebted to Miss Witherspoon as well. When we have Mathuin back we will all have reason to celebrate."

That evening, I shared with my fellow conspirators all that Rowena had told me. Wilo was sure that we had what we needed to make our plan successful. There wouldn't be much holding her back now. But I had one more thing I wanted to clear up before we initiated our offensive. With any luck, I now thought it was possible to find Mathuin and remove him from the prison, but what if Feardorcha decided to follow us? I felt we needed a way to capture Feardorcha in order to put an end once and for all to the terror he had put us all through. Our plans didn't address this as a possibility and I felt any victory we had, short of capturing Feardorcha, would only be temporary.

I hadn't seen or heard from my Mother since the night of our defeat of Feardorcha's troops, when she had driven the fire and the rain to our benefit. Tonight, as I prepared to sleep, I thought of her. I pictured her lovely face and I prayed like never before that she would come to me with an answer.

CHAPTER 32

AT LAST

Oona carried a golden birdcage that glowed like a lantern, to light her way as she descended the stone staircase. The cage looked very much like the one that I had rescued Wilo from, when this whole story began. Inside the cage was a bird, with glossy, black, iridescent feathers. Tied to the top of the cage, on the inside, was a holly branch. The black bird would open his beak to sing and a croak came out, followed by toads that hopped from his open beak and dropped from between the bars of the cage and down the well-worn steps, to a room at the very bottom of the castle, lit only by the glowing cage. A small round door opened to a tunnel under the thick castle walls. The light of day beckoned from the end of that tunnel, a slice of grass and sky. The toads were drawn to the promise of freedom at the end of the tunnel. They climbed over each other to reach it. Then, one by one, as if under the power of a trance, they hopped to the edge of a well and plunged headlong in. Unseen hands rolled a capstone over the top of the well, closing it off, with the toads inside. Oona continued to the edge of the cliff, holding the cage aloft. She swung the cage and the bird out over the crashing waves, and let go. It plunged into the dark waters below, the glow finally disappearing in the depths.

I related this latest dream of mine to the group gathered around the oak stump.

"It's a good sign that the dream came to you the night before we planned to bring Mathuin home," said Wilo. Then we joined hands, focused our thoughts, and directed them toward Mathuin.

As our eyes adjusted to the dim light, the tower room appeared just as Wilo had described it to us. Two foot thick stone walls, narrow windows; too narrow for a person to pass through, tapestries and iron sconces on the wall. A writing desk near the east-facing window, a narrow bed against the opposite wall, and on the bed, beneath Wilo's gaze as she lowered herself to one knee at the head of it, our Mathuin. A somewhat altered Mathuin, hair and beard long, limbs thinner and face paler than the Mathuin of our memories. Wilo's silvery-blond hair formed a curtain over their faces as she leaned down to touch his lips with hers. Tears escaped her eyes and fell upon his chest. Mathuin stirred and whispered her name.

"I'm here with you Mathuin, I'm right here."

His arms reached out for her, his left arm fell short in mid air, tethered as it was to a chain and anvil on the floor beside the bed. Mathuin's eyes flew open and he sat upright. He clutched the weeping Wilo to his chest, as his eyes took in each of us in turn, with an expression that changed like liquid mercury from disbelief, to joy, and then alarm.

"You shouldn't have come. Feardorcha won't let you leave here. He has plans for you Wilo."

"Well, he is not the only one with a plan," said Wilo. "We were hoping to leave here directly, but that would have been too simple. The chain and anvil will have to come off before we can transport you."

"There is a smithy on the bottom level of the castle. They took me there to give me my 'jewelry' after my last escape attempt," offered Mathuin.

"I am going to guess that there is at least one guard outside that door," I said.

"Two," responded Mathuin.

I felt for the colored powders at my waist and dumped the blue one into a metal pitcher of water on a stand by the window.

"I think they are probably tired and would appreciate a rest." I said as I knocked on the door.

The first guard cursed and approached the door. He slid the bar that opened the peephole and got a splash of colored water in his eyes. He immediately began rubbing his eyes, then stumbling in disorientation. The second guard opened the door and got the rest of the water square in his face. Within just a few minutes they were both slumped inertly on the floor and we were headed out the door, Mathuin carrying the anvil and chain. The narrow spiral staircase had well worn stone steps. It was so narrow that we needed to descend one at a time.

We surprised a maid coming up the stairs with food for the captive and guards. A sprinkling of the green powder and the frightened girl was chatting like we were her new best friends.

"Where is Feardorcha?" I demanded.

"Master is in the great hall entertaining guests. The duck is especially tasty tonight, everyone said so, and the pudding smells so good. The head cook is putting on airs about it, but it's much better than when master is displeased. Maybe we'll get a bit of it if there is anything left. We can always hope for that. Say, are you newly arrived here? If you are, misses, one of you will be sharing a room with a me. Which of you is the new maid and which the kitchen help? If you young gentlemen are to be stable hands then you are really lost here! You should be getting off to the stable before you are caught out of place. Your quarters will be out there."

"I'm the new maid, I'll take that meal to the prisoner, as I assume that is what you are carrying under that cloth. You may get to your leisure time a bit earlier tonight." This said by Cailean.

"Why thank you miss. I do appreciate it. I never look forward to the time the guards give me when I deliver the prisoner his meals. And I'd be surprised if he gets much of what I bring. I hear them joking about it as they look over what's on his tray. Though I must say he is sent much better than what prisoners usually are given. I've often been curious about who he is and what he has done to deserve his imprisonment."

The maid skipped off to her quarters with this assurance; "Don't worry, I won't mention you were out of place young sirs, just hurry yourselves to the stables before you are found out. Those in charge here can be very particular about propriety."

She left us the tray, which Cailean set beside the guards. Then we proceeded down the stairs.

The level of the great hall was abounding with good spirits. There was a celebration of some kind in progress; toasts being made, music played, laughter, and the confusion of many voices. With any luck there would be no notice of a small group slipping surreptitiously down the outer staircase. One by one we made the pass across the small dim space at the ground floor where our passage might be observed. One more level to go, worried that at any moment we would be detected, expecting at any moment that we would be.

Again luck was with us, the smithy was unmanned, tools laid out in orderly fashion, bellows at rest, fire extinguished. We discussed the options, it seemed there were two: the quicker noisier method; to smash the chain which would probably take several blows, or the quieter slower method; to light the fire and heat the metal until it was malleable. We decided to hedge our bets by starting the fire, and reserve the other option for necessity. Wilo stood guard, while I manned the bellows. Cailean fed the fire. The anvil end of the chain began to glow deep red. When the chain began to heat up at the level of Mathuin's wrist, we wrapped the manacle and his wrist in a gunny sack, and poured water over it to cool it. The anvil end of the chain was now cherry red. All it would take was one well-aimed blow to release Mathuin from the anvil. I stood up with the sledge hammer raised above my head, to deliver the blow. Before I could bring it down, it flew from my hands, and smashed against the wall. Feardorcha stood in the middle of the room, his face harboring a malevolent grin.

Then he spoke; "Oona's Wizard! My worthy adversary! I've been expecting you. What took you so long?"

Wilo dashed to pick up the hammer, and finish the job I had been prevented from doing.

Feardorcha watched her with an amused smile on his face. "Your devotion is very touching my dear. In fact I was counting on it. But let's not get carried away."

Feardorcha casually extended his arm, and with the slightest flick of his wrist, Wilo was flung against the wall, the hammer flying from her grasp.

Feardorcha had never turned his attention away from me, but now I felt the full intensity of his gaze. "There are those who would suggest that you are the greater wizard, young man. I, for one, have never believed you had more than luck at your disposal. You, of course, are the only one who knows the answer to this question; do you think your luck holds out? Or do you have more tricks you would like to show me? More bats or trained animals to employ? Perhaps you would like to have me forget our past encounters, and end this, by swearing allegiance to me now. You seem to have quite a following among the more ignorant villagers. If you swear your fealty now, we might be able to work something out, to all our advantage."

I lifted my gaze, from where Wilo lay in the corner trying to sit up, to meet the dark intensity of the wizard's glare. Senses heightened, I was aware of Cailean creeping silently in the shadows toward the hammer. As she reached to pick it up, I lurched toward Feardorcha in a clumsy pretense of obeisance. I reached to catch myself from stumbling and my free hand flew up and forward releasing the red powder which cascaded around Feardorcha's head and shoulders. Because he had misread my intentions, he had for one precious moment been fooled into not reacting to the threat. That is all it took. The hammer in Cailean's hand came down on the chain attached to the anvil, freeing Mathuin at last.

The four of us were reunited in an embrace, and a whispered destination. For one last instant we stood together, observing Feardorcha. His face was twisted in a grimace, his arms flailing at some unseen enemy, before we disappeared from that room.

Then we were with Fiona and Solomon in Siobhan's garden, and the final portion of our plan was set into play. We only had a limited amount of time before the effects of the red powder wore off. We were grateful for the time spent previously in preparation. Solomon and his soldiers were sent to line the beach facing the island fortress, preventing escape to the mainland. The only other escape would be from the cliff side to the crashing waves below. Rowena and her archers were sent for and placed strategically among the soldiers. In Siobhan's Garden, Mathuin and Wilo were preparing for Feardorcha's appearance. Mathuin was having the manacle and chain removed from his wrist and I heard him call for a sword to be found for him. Solomon waited with the rest of his soldiers, surrounding the garden.

I prepared myself mentally to transport back to the castle alone. If I returned before the effects of the powder were worn off I might just have a chance to eliminate Feardorcha.

I thought of Wilo's long sadness and separation from Mathuin. I didn't want them risking that journey again after being so recently reunited. I thought of my mother,

Oona, and the wonder of her friendship with Siobhan. I thought of Rozanna and her betrayal by Feardorcha, and of Fiona, their daughter, and marveled at the secrets Wilo had kept to protect her. I made my peace with my doubts and limitations. I prayed for strength for Cailean if I didn't return. I was consoled by the thought that I would soon be with my mother, and able to watch over my friends with her. I asked my mother to guide me, and my Creator to give me strength.

In a flash I was back inside the fortress, and to my surprise and relief, with me stood Oona, Siobhan and Rozanna. They were all dressed in blinding white with holly leaves in their flowing hair, and each wore a cape of red-gold netting. Their hands were joined together encircling Fiona, dressed as they were; all in white.

The Guardians had been busy too. While Fiona slept the trio had been watching over her at night. From the red-gold strands of hair Oona removed from Fiona's hairbrush each night, they had been weaving a delicate net as fine as a spider's web. They had been preparing for Feardorcha also.

The crowd of soldiers and archers watched from the shore in stunned silence as a long stream of vile creatures began a steady hemorrhage from all of the nooks and crannies of the fortress, heading like lemmings to the cliffs above the sea.

Then emerging from the bowels of the castle, led by Fiona, the three guardians; hands joined above their heads forming a cage of golden netting encircling Feardorcha, and containing him with a power he couldn't break; a power he had given up for what he mistakenly thought was a power greater than the power of love.